TARGET FOR MURDER

Angel Báez was 5'10" and built like a Mack Truck. He wore tight jeans and a tank top that showed off his muscles.

Aisha couldn't help but notice his bulging arms right away. Angel's nose had been broken at one time and Aisha saw a nasty scar that ran along his forehead just above one of his eyes.

"What can I do for you?" Angel asked in a slightly accented voice.

Aisha stood straight and showed no fear. She looked the man dead in the eyes.

"I want you to help me kill someone. I want you to help me kill Gary Steel."

A Gary Steel Mystery

Steel's Mettle

TEXT BY C. EMERSON

To John Herschel Glenn, Jr.

1921 – 2016

The first American to orbit the Earth . . . .

Published by:

Sedna Publishing Group

Plymouth, Devon, UK ▪ Springfield, Virginia, USA.

Internal layout and typesetting by Ian Regan.

.

Steel's Mettle

PROLOGUE

1986

Blessed.

That's what Percy Willow was, although he'd disagree with you about the suggestion of divine intervention. He'd argue he'd worked hard for his successes, and that he'd done it all by himself.

The truth was, it hadn't hurt that he'd been born a white male in 1950s America.

It could be said that he'd had a tough childhood because his parents had gifted him with a moniker that sounded like a derogatory term for a man's toughness, or the nickname of a certain part of the female anatomy. And that constantly being called that name while growing up had warped his mind.

But that'd be a lie.

He hadn't been called that. Not once. Not even in jest.

In reality, Percy had been very popular in school. People liked him and they were drawn to Percy like moths to a flame.

He had the type of personality and magnetism that made people just want to be his friend.

Percy had been a star athlete at Annandale High School where he'd been the quarterback on the football team and the captain of the baseball team.

He'd been the senior class president. And, in a non-academic accomplishment that he was proud of, he'd lost his virginity at 15 to the 18-year-old captain of the cheerleaders.

So, no: no one ever called him 'Pussy' Willow. That wasn't why he was warped.

Percy was tall, good-looking, athletic, smart, with a disarming smile and great sense of humor.

You could say he was George Clooney before George Clooney.

Unlike many of his peers, Percy hadn't been drafted into the military, so he'd never served in Vietnam in the 1960s or 70s.

He hadn't ducked it. He'd just been lucky and never received the call.

Instead, he went to the University of Virginia, the college Thomas Jefferson had founded in Charlottesville, Virginia.

He graduated *magna cum laude* in 1972 with a degree in finance.

Percy then moved to New York City where he started work for a prestigious Wall Street firm.

After a few years, he moved back to the Washington D.C. metropolitan area and opened his own consulting agency.

By the time he'd turned thirty, he was a millionaire several times over. He had a son by his trophy wife, Angela, and had accomplished everything he wanted to.

Well, except for one thing. You see, Percy was bored and wanted a challenge. He wanted to commit the perfect murder.

The idea had occurred to him after watching the Alfred Hitchcock movie, *Strangers on a Train.*

The plot was about a man who thinks he's come up with a way to perform the perfect murder. His plan was simple. Two strangers meet and agree to kill someone the other person wants dead. Basically switching motives and never seeing the other person again.

But Percy didn't want to bring someone else in on his murder. In his mind, having an extra person would be a liability and possibly a flaw.

Instead, he wanted to do it himself.

Johnny Cash summed it up best in *Folsom Prison Blues:* "I shot a man in Reno just to watch him die".

Ironically, Percy realized that his heart pumped a little harder and he felt a little more alive when he plotted someone else's death.

It was in late 1986 when he decided to give his obsession the good old college try.

The newest Washington D.C. Metrorail stop was in Vienna, Virginia. The Orange line had opened up there in June of that year.

The reason he chose that stop was because they didn't have security cameras up and working yet.

And who'd be stupid enough to kill someone on camera?

Well, maybe for fun he would, some day.

Percy had parked his car in Vienna and rode the Metrorail to the Metro Center stop in D.C.

A few hours later, he got back on the Metro and took a seat.

There were two women seated in front of him and he couldn't help but hear them talking.

"How's the new job going?" the heavyset blonde asked the skinny, short haired brunette.

"I hate it. I took the job to do math, not write reports. I hate writing! Numbers are my life!"

Poor girl, Percy thought. *She used the word hate twice in three sentences. She must be miserable! Well, sweetie, I can take care of that!*

He smiled and hoped that she'd ride the Metro to the end of the line.

He smiled again. *The end of the line . . .*

"Well, is Donnie at least taking care of you? You know, helping you work the stress out?"

The brunette leaned in.

"He's too small down below to do anything for me. I need a real man to make me feel good. With Donnie, I just fake it."

"Well, Penny, at least you've got someone!" the blonde giggled.

At the first stop, Percy got up and moved away from the two women. He'd picked out his victim. He now needed to stay away from her.

He watched her from a distance.

Penny was in her mid-to-late twenties. She was cute enough. Percy didn't particularly like her short permed brown hair. Her best assets were her boobs. She was stacked.

Percy looked at them.

It's a pity to waste such a nice piece of ass.

But it was too late for her. He'd already decided. She was dead.

Percy put his hands inside his coat pocket and put his fingers around a small handgun. It felt cold to the touch. He felt his heart start to beat harder.

At each stop, Percy held his breath and anxiously watched Penny. But to his relief, she didn't get off.

Finally, they were all headed for the final stop.

When they got there, the train slowed down and came to rest. The doors slid open and Percy hung back as the two women got up. Then he followed them out.

The Vienna Metro line was located on the median strip of Interstate 66. Percy watched as the two women said goodbye and separated. The blonde walked south on the elevated walkway over the westbound highway. Peggy headed north over the eastbound traffic.

Percy stayed back on the platform, pretending to take in the view of the passing cars. Then when he felt he'd given Peggy enough of a lead, he hustled after her.

I can't believe my luck. She's headed toward the lot where I parked my car. The getaway should be a breeze!

Yes, Percy Willow seemed to lead a charmed life.

Percy watched as Peggy stopped at her car door to pull the keys from her purse.

He took one last look around. All clear. No one was nearby. He held his breath as he glided silently across the concrete parking lot.

He reached into his coat and grabbed his gun.

She didn't notice him.

He pulled it free.

Peggy got her keys out and worked one into the car door.

Percy put the gun to her head. She turned towards him, surprised.

He pulled the trigger.

She never knew what hit her. Without making a sound she crumpled to the ground like a house of cards.

Percy didn't take time to watch. Instead, he pivoted and calmly walked away.

His nerves were jumpy. The gunshot had been louder than he'd anticipated.

But no one seemed to notice.

I feel so alive!

With his heart racing, Percy walked to his car and drove home.

ONE

Once again I found myself in Vietnam with my Navy SEAL team. We were set up along the banks of the Cu Lao Ca Xuc for an ambush.

I could hear my heart pounding deep in my ears as a sampan suddenly appeared, floating downriver. I steadied my breath and readied my aim. The instant Lieutenant Shaffer opened fire, my trigger finger would twitch and "Big Momma," my Stoner 63 machine gun, would belch its one-way ticket to hell.

I could see three North Vietnamese Army Soldiers in green uniform on board. One was standing next to the small shelter in the middle of the sampan.

I realized that there could be more NV inside.

"Lai dai!" (Come here!) Lt. Shaffer yelled.

The NVA soldiers looked at one another in shock. They didn't seem to believe that the enemy had penetrated into the middle of their swamp.

"Lai dai! Lai dai!" screamed Lt. Shaffer again.

The VC continued to stare dumbly at us as the sampan started to float out of range.

"Lai dai, dammit!" cried the Lieutenant in frustration. "I said get over here!"

The soldiers took one last look at each other and then they dove into the water. The SEAL team immediately opened up with a barrage of firepower.

As it rained bullets on the river, a movement caught my eye. Someone was coming out from the little wooden shelter on the sampan. My finger tensed. I wasn't about to let the enemy get off any shots at my brothers.

So, as the figure emerged, Big Momma roared.

But I realized too late that the figure was a woman– and she was carrying a bundle.

She slumped over against the little shelter in the boat. I'd shot her numerous times. Then, to my horror, I heard a baby's cry.

I dropped my gun and dove into the cold river. I swam as hard as I could after the floating sampan. By now the heartbeat in my ears thundered like a bass drum.

I could hear the baby crying loudly over the gunfire.

It was screaming bloody murder!

I closed the gap on the boat and pulled myself onboard.

I quickly pulled the dead woman's bloody body aside and saw the now dead baby boy ravaged with bullet holes from my gun.

"Nooooo!" I screamed as I fell to my knees.

I shot up in bed like a jack-in-the-box.

I'd been dreaming. Or maybe I should say I'd been having my recurring nightmare again.

I sat there in the dark with my head in my hands. I was tangled up in my sheets, saturated with sweat.

Tears streamed down my face and I wiped them away with the back of my hand.

It'd been a while since I'd had my nightmare. I knew it was because of what happened yesterday: while out running, I'd stopped to watch a group of young men playing basketball. They were in their twenties: the same age as the boy I'd killed on that river would've been today.

"I've gotta stop doing that," I said quietly to myself, referring to watching people his age.

I had never forgiven myself for killing that child. But over time, I'd slowly realized that I couldn't keep beating myself up for it either.

I looked at the clock on my bedside table. The soft yellow glow of the light read 4:32.

I'd been here before. I wasn't going to be able to fall back to sleep anytime soon. And since I was planning to get up in half an hour to go for a run and have a workout, I just got up.

TWO

Monday, June 7, 1993

I got in a good run that morning. I drove into D.C. and ran around the National Mall. As usual, I stopped by the Vietnam Veterans Memorial to pay respect to my fallen brothers.

I usually ran with my good friend, Joe Wilson. He was a detective with the Fairfax County Police Department. But his son had recently been murdered and he and his wife Carolyn were still feeling their way through the tragedy.

Joe would be back out running with me soon enough. If not, I'd drag his ass out and make him do it.

I worked out in my gym, which was located in the basement of my split level home in Springfield, Virginia. It's a great gym. With inset lighting and mirrors on the wall, it was equipped with a universal weight system, lots of free weights for dumb-bells and barbells; it also had kettlebells, a treadmill, punching bag, and a speed bag.

And of course a great sound system that shook the walls when I cranked it up!

After my workout, I showered and ate breakfast.

The fog from my abrupt awakening earlier that morning had long since dissipated by the time I finally walked back down-stairs to my office.

Yes, I worked from home. And let me tell you, the commute was murder.

Not!

After I'd gotten out of the Navy, I'd searched for a job that would get me out and about. I knew I would never be happy as a desk jockey.

I'd decided to try and be a private investigator. And you know what? I've never regretted it!

Don't get me wrong. Being a P.I. can be about as exciting as watching paint dry, especially when you're sitting in a car overnight on a stakeout. But it also offered a variety of cases, not unlike executing different missions as a Navy SEAL.

This morning, around nine o'clock, I found myself sitting in the office reading the sports section of the *USA Today.* Out of the corner of my eye I noticed a movement on one of the monitors of my security camera. I turned and watched as a car pulled up to the front curb of the house.

I instantly recognized the car. It belonged to Leigh Ellerton.

Leigh was a friend of mine who worked at the DMV.

People say that you can't be friends with someone of the opposite sex without one of them wanting more.

Well, in this case they were absolutely right!

Leigh was my beautiful dream girl. But it was not to be.

Leigh was married with three kids. She stood five-foot-four and possessed the dangerous curves of a mountain road. She had blue eyes, high cheekbones, and a flawless smile. Her face was framed by her long, layered, strawberry-blonde hair.

To sum it up, she took my breath away!

But she was more than just a looker. Leigh was intelligent, kind, and had a great sense of humor.

I wasn't sure why she was stopping by now. I'd recently offered her a job as my secretary, but she'd turned it down.

She was happy working as a manager down at the telephone company.

So at the moment, I didn't have a secretary. But I still had a contact down at the phone company who could run telephone numbers for me.

I watched her stride up the sidewalk. She was wearing a dark skirt, white blouse, with slight heels.

Beautiful!

I stood up, walked out of my office, and into the lobby.

I got to the front door just as she arrived.

"Good morning," I said, opening the door before she could ring the bell.

"Hi, Gary. Do you have a minute?"

"For you? Sure."

That's it. Play it cool.

She came in and I led her back into my office.

She took a seat while I walked behind my desk and sat down.

"Would you like something to drink?" I asked. "Water?"

"That'd be nice," she answered. "Thank you."

I reached over and opened my mini-fridge.

"Here you go," I said as I handed her a bottle. I grabbed one for myself and opened it. "I assume this isn't a social call?"

"No, it's not."

Leigh took a long draw on the bottle. She was obviously upset.

Finally she said, "A friend of mine, Becky Whitfield, who I've known since high school, was arrested last night for murder."

Without thinking, I leaned forward in my chair.

"I know she didn't do it!" Leigh continued.

"How do you know?" I asked.

"Because she's charged with murdering her own son. His name is," she stopped and corrected herself, "was, Cody."

Well, that stopped me dead in my tracks.

"How old was he and how'd he die?"

"He was sixteen and he was stabbed to death."

"How many times was he stabbed?" I asked, feeling like a prize-winning jerk.

"Five."

I nodded my head and we sat quietly for a moment while I absorbed what she'd said.

Filicide is the deliberate act of a parent killing their child. It comes from some Latin words. Filicide can refer to either the crime or the perpetrator.

I recalled reading a recent study that concluded that mothers were responsible for a higher share of murdered infants. Fathers were more likely to have killed children aged eight or older.

"Okay, Leigh," I said as I pulled open a desk drawer and pulled out a legal writing pad and pen. I was ready to take notes. "Tell me exactly what happened."

"Well, Becky and her husband, Ted, separated last year. It was because of Becky's drug problem. She'd been a partier since college and I figured she'd outgrow it. She has three kids after all!"

Leigh stopped.

"Two kids now," she said sadly.

She was rambling a bit. But at the moment, I was going to let her tell her tale her way.

"Umm, anyway," Leigh continued. "Ted filed for divorce and they've been in a nasty custody fight over the kids ever since. Cody stays with Becky right now."

She stopped. "I mean he stayed with Becky because he didn't want to change high schools. The younger two children live with their dad."

I'd never seen Leigh like this before. She was rattled. Usually she was always in control.

"Last Saturday night, Cody went out with some friends. Becky stayed home and got high."

"On what?" I asked, figuring it was pot.

Leigh hesitated and then said, "Heroin."

I shook my head. Becky was using hardcore!

"She swears she passed out in the living room. She was watching TV. But when she woke up she was in her bedroom on her bed, naked. And Gary, she doesn't sleep naked, especially with kids around.

"Becky says she got up around four in the morning to go to the bathroom. Afterwards she went to Cody's bedroom to check and see if he'd gotten home okay. She found him in bed, stabbed to death."

Leigh started to cry.

"Gary, he was such a good kid! He was a straight A student. He played varsity football as a sophomore and this spring was awarded an internship on Capitol Hill. He wanted to go to an Ivy League school."

Leigh sobbed.

"He was going to be somebody special!"

I reached behind my desk and grabbed a box of Kleenex. I handed it to her.

"Thank you."

I watched her wipe her tears. I wanted to get up and go over and hold her.

But I didn't.

"And Becky would never hurt him, much less kill him! She was proud of him. She loved him!"

"What happened next?" I asked, trying to keep things moving.

"Becky dialed 911. An ambulance came, but Cody was already dead. The police investigated and found Becky's fingerprints all over the kitchen knife that was used."

"Was it her kitchen knife?"

"Yes," Leigh answered weakly. "They also found blood all over her clothes. They'd been tossed into a pile behind her bed against the wall."

Leigh looked at me pleadingly. "Gary, I know how it looks. But she didn't do it!"

I nodded my head.

"Tell me, Leigh, have you ever noticed any signs that the children had been physically abused?"

"What? No! Never!"

I'd asked the question because research suggested that children who'd been murdered by their parents usually had also been physically abused prior to death.

"And here," Leigh said. "Here's a Christmas card with a family picture on it. It was so nice I couldn't throw it away."

She handed it to me. "Happier times."

"Thanks," I said as I took it.

It was a normal picture-card. The family had dressed up and gone to a photographer. They'd posed in front of a sparkling Christmas tree with a fake window with snow on the glass.

"Merry Christmas from the Whitfields!" was printed on the side of the picture.

I looked at the oldest boy, Cody. He was a good looking kid. He had dark hair, a nice smile, and a dimple in his chin.

"Okay," I said, tossing the pen onto the legal pad. "I'll take a look into it."

"How much?" she asked.

"No charge," I said.

She started to protest but I held my hand up cutting her off.

"It's what friends do. Leigh, you've helped me out by running numbers and getting addresses more times than I can count and I appreciate it."

"But it's not the same thing," she protested.

"No charge," I said again.

"Okay," she said reluctantly. "Thank you."

Leigh looked up at me and smiled. It broke my heart.

For her sake, I hoped her friend hadn't done it!

THREE

Aisha Nader guided her rust-colored 1989 Ford Escort 3-door hatchback off I-395 and onto the Glebe Road exit. She was nervous and she reached over and grabbed ahold of her Berretta handgun, which was lying on the passenger seat.

It'll be okay. They hate him too.

Aisha was born and raised in the United States. But she'd helped the Liberation Army's Fifth Battalion—a terrorist group who'd attacked the World Trade Towers in February—in an attempted nuclear attack on Washington D.C. just a few weeks previously in May.

Now, Aisha's boyfriend—the married leader of the sect, Ramzi Sheikh Mohammed—was behind bars, never to see daylight again.

He'd sent her a note as to the reason the attack failed:

**The infidel's name is Gary Steel. He lives in
Springfield. He's a private investigator.
But be cautious my love.
I believe in reality he is U.S. military.
May the vengeance of Allah rain down upon him as
Al Muntaqim, The Avenger, uses you as his vessel!
Allah be with you!**

The message was clear and she understood. Aisha would be cautious as she exacted revenge.

She'd researched Gary Steel in the *Washington Post.* She'd been surprised to find a fair amount of stories about him. One in particular piqued her interest. It was from November of last year. Steel had broken up a drug ring that'd been smuggling fentanyl from Fairfax and other local hospitals. What caught her attention was that members of the Chirilaguas, a gang made up of El Salvador youths, had also been implicated in the drug bust.

Being Muslim, Aisha didn't endorse drug use. In fact she detested it. But she was looking for an ally to go up against Steel.

The enemy of my enemy is my friend.

Through the articles, she'd learned that Gary Steel was a former Navy SEAL. She could tell by the one picture she'd seen that he was a big man, probably around 6'4". He was also built like an NFL middle linebacker.

His muscles have muscles.

Aisha couldn't help but notice that Steel was also very handsome.

It's too bad you must die!

She'd thought of setting up an appointment at his detective agency, walking in, and shooting him in the head. But she didn't know the layout of the office, nor did she know how many other people might be working with him.

She thought of trying to seduce him. But she knew the more she was seen with him, the more she'd be a suspect.

Because Steel was such a powerful man and obviously not dumb, Aisha had decided to see if she could enlist the Chirilaguas' help in exacting her revenge.

She turned down Mt. Vernon Avenue and crossed a bridge. Then, she drove slowly along the strip malls that lined either side of the street.

She saw a group of young Hispanic-looking men dressed in black standing on a street corner.

Aisha parked her car.

She stuck her Beretta M9 gun in the waistband of her sweatpants. She'd purposely dressed down for the encounter. Her black hair was pulled back in a ponytail. She wore no makeup and, despite it being hot outside, she hid her girlish figure underneath a baggy sweatshirt.

Aisha got out of her car and walked toward the three men.

Despite her attempt at dressing down, she couldn't hide her beauty or her tall, willowy body.

She got their attention right away,

"*Hola chica. Te ves bien! ¿Quieres follar?*" the biggest one said.

That got a laugh all around, and Aisha figured he'd just said something crude.

She ignored it. Instead she looked at the youth. He was in his early twenties. He was tall, but chubby. He had black hair that was shaved tight on the sides but flopped down longer on top. Aisha noted 'Chirilaguas' was tattooed on his bicep above a depiction of a skull.

Perfect!

"I was wondering if you could help me? I've got a proposition for your leader."

"I've got a proposition for you, *mamacita*," the man said, grabbing his crotch and tugging at it.

The other two laughed and made kissing noises.

"Do you know Gary Steel?" she asked.

Javier Hernández immediately stopped laughing. "Yeah? What about him?"

"He's a mutual enemy and I want to talk to the head of your gang about him."

Javy shot a look at the other two. The look warned them to not tell this woman that Steel had been instrumental in the arrest of his baby brother, Fernando.

"*El Jefe,*" said the smallest one, using the Spanish word for *the boss,* "doesn't like visitors."

"Maybe if we bring him this piece of ass he'll be all right with it," the other chimed in.

The two looked at Javy. It was his decision.

"Listen lady," Javy said. "I can't guarantee your safety. *El Jefe* takes what he wants."

Aisha stood there for a moment. She was scared, but trying hard not to show it. If she hadn't been packing a gun, she would've run away from the situation as fast as she could!

"That's all right," she said, her voice sounding calm. "I can take care of myself."

Javy flicked his head side-to-side. "It's your call, *mamacita.*"

"Let's go," she said firmly.

"I'll drive you."

"I've got a car."

"I said, I'll drive."

It wasn't an offer.

"Okay."

The four of them piled into an old ratty brown Chevy. Javy turned the key and the car's engine coughed and sputtered. Finally, it backfired and roared to life.

They were off.

As Javy drove down the street, Aisha tried to remember her way. But after a few turns, she was lost.

Finally they turned down a dead end street. The street sign had been painted over and said: Lucifer Lane.

They drove to the end of the road to number 209.

Aisha was surprised. The house wasn't as run down as she'd expected. In fact, the house looked nice.

Javy pulled up and parked on the street facing the yellow, colonial house.

"You sure about this Javy?" one of the guys asked.

"Yeah, I'm sure. Steel took money from our pockets. Angel (he pronounced it On-hel) and I have been talking about finding a way to return the favor."

The four got out of the car. But instead of walking up to the front door, Javy led the group around to the back of the house.

There, they found a sliding glass door with the drapes drawn closed.

Javy rapped out a sequence on the glass.

Knock, knock-knock, knock, knock-knock-knock.

A moment passed and then the curtain was pulled back.

A man who had a face like a clenched fist stood there, scowling. He saw Javy and opened the door.

"*¿Qué pasa? Sabes que no me gusta que la gente venga a mi casa.*"

"I know. I'm sorry. She knows Gary Steel and wants our help."

The man stood there for a moment, contemplating what'd been said. Then he nodded his head and slid the door all the way open.

"Come in," he said.

Aisha went in first. Javy followed. When the other two started to come in, the man held up his hand and closed the door.

They stayed outside.

Aisha found herself in a furnished basement. A television was on with the sound down. On the table, in front of an old beaten up sofa, was a half-eaten sandwich. A bag of potato chips lay open beside it.

"This is the *El Jefe*, Angel," Javy said as they all stood facing one another.

Angel Báez was 5'10" and built like a Mack Truck. He wore tight jeans and a tank top that showed off his muscles.

Aisha couldn't help but notice his arms right away.

Probably hardened from years spent in prison.

Angel's nose had been broken at one time and Aisha saw a nasty scar that ran along his forehead just above one of his eyes.

Upon closer inspection, she was surprised to realize that this man was probably in his late twenties, as was she.

"What can I do for you?" Angel asked in a slightly accented voice.

Aisha stood straight and showed no fear. She looked the man dead in the eyes.

"I want you to help me kill someone. I want you to help me kill Gary Steel."

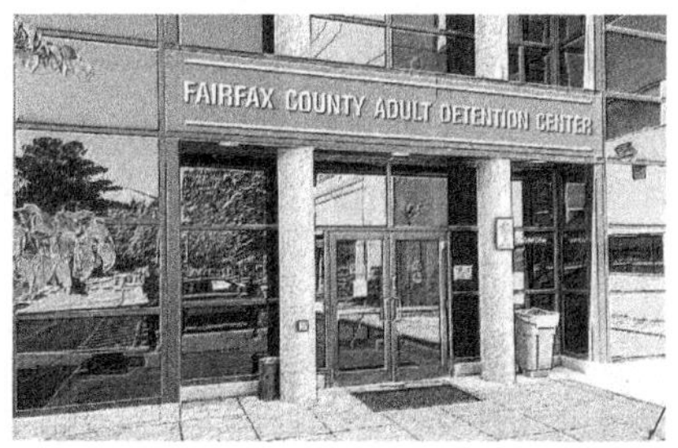

FOUR

I walked Leigh to her car and promised her I'd look into her case.

I stood at the curb and watched her drive off.

I waved like a little kid.

After making sure nobody saw that, I turned and went back into my office and locked up. I then walked through the house and into the garage. There, I kept my two cars parked. One, my baby, was a red, 1991 Chevrolet Corvette ZR-1. It was sweet!

You could say it was my mid-life crisis car. But I'd owned a Corvette since I was twenty-one.

So I guess I'd been in my mid-life crisis for a couple of decades now!

The other car was a neon green, 1989 Ford Taurus wagon. This was the one I tended to use when working a case or following a subject. Despite its color, it looked like a ton of other cars out on the road and it easily blended in.

Today though, I selected my Corvette.

Leigh had told me that her friend was expecting me. Becky was being held at the Fairfax County Adult Detention Center.

'Detention Center' was just a fancy name for jail.

Since inmates were allowed to have confidential, unscheduled visits with attorneys and other professionals, I didn't need to schedule an appointment.

I sat and waited for about fifteen minutes while they went and brought Becky Whitfield to the visitation room.

The place had ten small tables with chairs. One big beefy guard stood posted at the door, observing everything.

As I sat at my table, I noted that three of the other tables were filled. For the most part, the people sitting at them leaned in towards each other and talked in hushed tones.

I guess they tried to make the visitation room cheery. The bare cinderblock walls were painted a forsythia shade of yellow. And despite the slight smell of antiseptic in the air, the place reeked of desperation.

I sat there patiently. Finally, the door opened and another guard led a woman in.

She was uncuffed. She walked slowly, her head down and shoulders slumped. The guard led her towards my table. When she finally looked up at me, I noticed that her eyes were red.

Becky was around 5'2" and, despite her condition, I could tell that she had a very pretty face. And like most middle-aged Americans, she was carrying a bit more weight than she should have. Her shoulder-length brown hair was disheveled and her pleasant face looked pale.

It didn't take a P.I. to realize that Becky Whitfield had been through hell.

She was wearing a red, one piece overall that had **Fairfax County Jail** stenciled on the back in block letters.

I stood up and pulled the seat out for her. It made a scuffling sound on the worn tile floor.

As she sat down, I pushed the seat in. Then I scootched back around and sat down.

"Hi, Becky," I said. "I'm Gary Steel."

I stuck my hand out and she shook it. Her hands were cold and clammy.

"Hi," she answered in a high, lilting voice.

I figured this wasn't the time for small talk. What was I going to say? "So how's the food?"

So instead, I just dove in.

"If it's possible, I'd like you to tell me exactly what happened."

She shook her head. "I don't really know," she replied meekly.

"Well, please try," I urged.

She nodded and said, "In a nutshell, I was watching TV, got high, and passed out. About six hours later, I woke up in my bed. When I did, I went and checked on my boy." She paused and shook her head in disbelief. Then she blurted out, "But he was dead."

She put her hands to her face and started to sob.

People looked over at us and stared.

I didn't care.

"I didn't do it!" she almost shouted. "I'd never hurt my son!"

"It's okay," I said calmly. "I believe you. I just need to get some more information so that I can prove it."

Becky nodded her head in understanding and waited.

"I'm going to ask you some questions and they might be hard to answer," I said as I pulled out a small flip top notepad from my pocket and grabbed a pen.

"Okay," she said, trying to compose herself.

But tears continued to roll down her cheeks.

"Do you usually take heroin?"

"Yes," she said, nodding her head sadly. "Usually on the weekends when I don't have custody of the kids."

I knew that was bullshit. Heroin was a highly addictive drug and it wasn't something you just did occasionally. But I was sure she was embarrassed and couldn't face telling me the truth, so I let it slide.

"Do you do it alone?" I asked.

"No. I usually take it with my boyfriend. We do it to take the edge off."

"Boyfriend?" I asked.

"Yes."

"What's his name?"

"Mitchell. Mitchell Jones."

I jotted that down.

"Was he there that night?"

"No. He was at an Orioles game with a friend."

The Baltimore Orioles played baseball about forty miles north of Washington D.C. The Senators had left D.C. at the end of the 1971 season and became the Texas Rangers. Major League Baseball had tried to pawn the Orioles off as our local team.

I didn't buy it. Most people didn't.

But if you wanted to see big league baseball, you had to go to Baltimore.

Becky wiped the tears from her cheeks with her hand.

"Okay," I continued. "Do you usually get so high that you pass out?"

I wasn't an expert on heroin. But I'd seen it enough in Vietnam to know a little about it.

Heroin was about numbing or avoiding pain. To me, it wasn't a recreational drug like alcohol, marijuana, cocaine, and meth. Heroin was for self-medication.

I figured Becky did it because of her marital situation. Divorce was bad enough. But throw in kids and you've just upped the emotional pain level exponentially.

Heroin causes chemical changes to flood the brain giving a person an intense feeling of pleasure.

It also changes thoughts.

Could it have caused her to kill?

"No. I've never passed out before. I might get drowsy, but nothing like what happened. I don't know what came over me," she said, throwing her hands up in exasperation. "One minute I was in the living room. The next thing I knew, hours had passed and I woke up in bed."

"Was the TV still on?"

She sat there for a moment. "No. No, I don't think it was."

"Do you recall turning it off?"

"No."

"Okay," I said, as I wondered if someone else might've been there. "Leigh told me you woke up naked."

Without thinking, she put her arms up in front of her breasts.

"I did. And I never sleep in the nude. I have kids and I would never do that!"

"Do you think you had sex?" I asked.

"What? No!" she said adamantly, her voice rising with anger.

I threw my hands up. "I'm not saying consensually, I'm just wondering if someone forced themselves on you while you were passed out. Or, maybe . . . maybe your boyfriend stopped by after the game."

Becky stopped still.

"I don't think so," she answered.

"I'm just trying to ascertain if someone else was there."

"Oh, okay. But I really don't think so."

"Do you know how blood got all over your clothes?"

I was hoping she'd say something like that she woke up, dressed, checked on her son. Saw him dead, took him into her arms, thus getting blood transfer. Then she got up, dialed 911 and then changed out of the bloody clothes.

But no such luck.

"No," she answered.

"Umm, do you think you almost overdosed?"

"No. I don't think so. I took a normal hit."

"Could anyone have messed with the heroin?"

"Again, I don't think so. I got it straight from my boyfriend. He stopped by earlier that day and gave it to me before he left that afternoon. There's no reason he would mess with the stuff."

I switched gears.

"Does Mitchell like your kids?"

"What? Yes. Of course he does. He's got a good relationship with Cody. In fact, he had someone help Cody get a big-time internship on Capitol Hill for Senator Frank Lindsey."

"Okay," I responded, "how about your husband. Does he like your kids? Cody?"

"He loves them! That's why he's fighting me so hard for custody."

"Is he the type of guy who thinks, 'Well, if I can't have them, no one can'?"

"No. Not at all!"

"Okay, does Cody have any enemies?"

Yes, it felt like a stupid question. But I had to ask it.

"Of course not," she snapped. "He's only sixteen and well liked."

"Look, I'm sorry Mrs. Whitfield. But I have to cover every possibility if I'm to get to the bottom of this."

"Yes, of course you do. I'm sorry."

"Any problems with the drug dealers?"

"No, we pay them as soon as we get the stuff."

"Can I have their names?"

"I don't know my guy, just where he hangs out."

"I'll take that."

She gave me the location; then described him to me.

"I don't want to get in trouble," she said.

"If I ever talk to him, he won't know you told me a thing."

I finished writing in my notebook. By now, I think I was just about through.

"Is there anything else you can tell me?" I asked. "Anything that seemed strange about that night? That day?"

Becky sat there, still as a statue, as she thought.

"No. Not a thing."

She looked at me.

"If you can give me the contact information for Mitchell," I said. "I do need to talk to him."

"I told you he didn't do it. He was at the game."

"I didn't say he did anything, Becky. But I still need to talk to him. He might know something."

Reluctantly, she gave me his information.

I could tell she really liked the guy and just didn't want to get him involved in this mess.

In the end she said, "Thank you for helping me. I just hope that after you clear me, the cops will start looking for the real murderer."

FIVE

Aisha didn't know what to expect, but she certainly didn't expect what happened next.

She'd just told Angel that she wanted help and he reached out and grabbed her.

In one quick motion he pulled her tight, then reached around and pulled the Beretta from her waistband.

"Never come into my house with a gun!" he spat in her face.

She almost gagged on his warm, peanut-butter breath.

Angel shoved her away.

Aisha watched as the man pushed the gun's release and pulled the magazine out. He pulled the slide back and the chambered bullet spun out of the top landed noiselessly on the rug.

Angel threw the magazine on the sofa.

"I have a daughter and wife who live here," he said angrily at Aisha.

He turned toward Javy and pointed the empty gun at his face.

"*Y idiota,* you know better. You check anyone you bring here to my home."

"Y-yes, s-sir," Javy stuttered. "I'm sorry."

Javy took the gun and tossed it too onto the sofa.

"Now we talk," Angel said. He motioned to a chair, "Take a seat."

Without her gun, Aisha felt vulnerable. She knew he could do whatever he wanted to her and she was scared. But she did

[37]

her best to hide it. She knew that animals sensed fear. So she sat down stony-faced. The two gang members looked at her expectantly.

Aisha had already decided that she couldn't tell them the truth. If they knew she'd been part of a terrorist cell, they might execute her. After all, they were Americans.

"Gary Steel was responsible for getting my cousin, Antonio, arrested on weapons charges."

Even though she knew she obviously looked Persian, Aisha had picked the fake name Antonio, hoping that the two men would think she was Italian. After all, she had olive skin and dark hair.

It could work. Americans are so gullible and ignorant.

"I want revenge," she continued as her voice rose. "I want the asshole dead! He ruined my aunt's family!"

This seemed to appease Angel.

"And why come to us?"

"I did some research on Steel. I was going to try and kill him myself. But I read in the newspaper that he'd helped the police bust some Chirilaguas in a drug ring last year."

"Yes, one of them was my brother!" Javy admitted.

Angel turned and shot him a piercing look that said, *Shut-up!*

"I hoped you might be willing to help me out," she said. "Steel is a former Navy SEAL. He's big, strong, and dangerous. I figured I could use all the help I could get."

Javy looked silently at his *Jefe*.

"Do you have anything specific in mind?" Angel asked.

"I just figured we'd go to his house, break in, and blow the man away."

Angel laughed and clapped his hands. "Remind me not to piss you off!"

The three sat there silently for a moment.

"I tell you what. I'll send some men with you. But the execution will be done Chirilaguas-style. That way people will get the message not to fuck with us!"

Aisha smiled. "Thank you."

She didn't know what 'Chirilaguas-style' was and she didn't care. All that mattered was that she'd talked the gang into doing her dirty work for her.

She closed her eyes for a moment.

Al Muntaqim, *the Avenger, thank you for letting me use these stupid Americans as your vessel. Allah be praised!*

SIX

Later that afternoon, after interviewing Becky Whitfield in jail, I found myself sitting in front of a row of brick townhouses in Fairfax, Virginia.

I'd decided to just "drop by" on her boyfriend, Mitchell Jones. I wanted to surprise him.

It's not that I suspected him. He didn't seem to have a motive and it appeared like he'd had an alibi, forty miles away.

But truth be told, as far as I was concerned, everyone was a suspect until they weren't.

I knew I might be in for a long wait, especially if he went out after work to do something. Something like visiting Becky in jail.

But it wasn't too bad of a wait, about an hour. Around 5:35, a 1992 Ford F-150 pulled up in his numbered parking space.

I got out of my car and started walking towards him.

It was a fairly new truck, but I thought it was ugly. It was red with a wide brown panel running along the sides.

Red and brown?

Oh well. I was never good at fashion anyway.

"Mr. Jones?" I asked as he stepped out of the truck.

"Yes?" he answered, looking at me uneasily.

Mitchell Jones was about six feet tall, thin, with handsome, chiseled features.

I was surprised at how young he looked. He appeared to be in his late twenties.

On the other hand, Becky looked to be in her forties.

On the surface, a middle-aged woman and a young stud didn't seem to make sense.

No matter how pretty the girl was.

But then again, I was certainly no expert when it came to love.

"Mitchell Jones?"

"Yes," he answered hesitantly.

"Hi, I'm Gary Steel. I'm looking into the Becky Whitfield case."

"Oh, yes!" he said relieved. "She told me some P.I. was going to try and help her out. You're friends with Leigh Ellerton?"

"Yes."

"Well, what can I do for you?"

"I'd like to ask you some questions about the night of the murder."

He shook his head. "Certainly. It was a terrible tragedy. Do you want to come in?"

"Sure."

He pulled the storm door to his townhouse open and unlocked the front door.

I followed him inside. His house was fairly neat and clean, at least for a guy.

To the right was a kitchen and on the table I saw a box of Cheerios, a folded newspaper, and an empty ashtray. Mitchell walked into the kitchen and dropped his keys into the ashtray.

"You want anything to drink?" he asked over his shoulder. "A beer?"

"No thanks, I'm good."

"Well, I'm gonna grab one."

While Jones opened the refrigerator, I took a quick look around.

I stood in a small hallway that led to the living room. Right next to me was a small table. On top of it was a game ticket from Oriole Park at Camden Yards. It was on top of a crisp, unopened Baltimore Orioles 1993 yearbook.

"You go see the Orioles much?" I asked.

"A fair amount," he answered. "I love the ballpark. Have you been there?"

"No, not yet. But I want to."

Camden Yards had opened the previous season. It was reportedly the most beautiful ballpark in baseball. It was even hosting this year's Major League Baseball's All-Star game next month.

"You ought to go," Mitchell said. "It's a great place to see a ballgame."

Mitchell had twisted the top off his beer and tossed it on the kitchen table. He motioned me to go into the living room. I went in and grabbed a seat on the sofa.

I noted the furniture seemed nice but used.

He had a few pictures on the wall. One was a painting of a Baltimore Colt done by Dave Boss. He'd been commissioned by the National Football League to do some team paintings in the 1960s. They'd been used for the cover of team yearbooks and sold as posters. I remember one of the Los Angeles Rams being hung on the wall in a barracks when I was in Vietnam.

This was the first time I'd seen one of the original paintings.

"That's nice," I said, gesturing to the picture.

I was trying to get him relaxed and talking. It's an interview technique I'd always found useful.

"Oh?" he said, looking. "No, that's just a paint embellished print. Even though it's about twenty-five years old, they're fairly common, thankfully, or I'd never be able to afford it."

"You a Colts fan?" I asked.

"I used to be. That is until they left town in '84 for Indianapolis. I remember my dad taking me to see a game when I was young. I got to see Johnny Unites play. I fell in love with him and the team that day."

I nodded my head. So much for small talk. It was time to get down to business.

But Mitchell beat me to it.

"So what can I do for you?" he asked.

"Well, I just need to verify some things," I answered, as I pulled out my notepad and pen.

"Sure."

"Becky said that you gave her the heroin she took that night."

Mitchell was bringing the bottle of beer up to his lips. He froze when I asked the question.

"Wow, I guess she isn't holding anything back."

I just looked at him.

He put his beer down.

"Yes, I got her the stuff. We usually get high together. The heroin leads to better sex. Becky loses her inhibitions and she seems to enjoy it more, too." He paused, looked at me, and smiled. "You know what I mean?"

As he said it, he lifted his eyebrows like Groucho Marx.

I nodded. I knew what he meant. Better orgasms. But he was wrong. It was a popular myth that heroin enhanced sex, but the truth of the matter was that heroin led to sexual dysfunction for both male and female users.

How do I know? Well, it's amazing the things you learn as a private investigator. Now, if he'd said ecstasy, I couldn't argue.

"Did you get it from your normal dealer?" I asked.

He looked hesitant to answer. I understood. He didn't want to get himself or his dealer in trouble.

"Yes," he finally answered. "Why?"

"Becky reacted to it differently than usual."

"I heard. I figured she took too much. Stupid! She could've died." He looked down. "I usually do the shooting up for us."

I nodded my head again. That made sense.

"So, Becky was alone because you went to the Orioles game that night?"

"Yes. It was a good game. The O's won 5-3. But now, after what happened, I wished I'd stayed with her. Maybe I could have prevented whatever happened."

"And after the game?"

"Oh, my buddy and I went drinking."

"Where?"

"Pickles Pub."

"How late did you stay?"

"Until closing."

"And what is your friend's name?"

"Wait a minute. Why are you asking? Am I a suspect?"

"No, just covering all bases." I stopped and looked him dead in the eye. "Do you have a problem with that?"

"No, no problem at all," he answered. "His name is Roger Penn. But please, keep it close to the vest. He's the Chief of Staff to United States Senator Frank Lindsey. I don't want to bring Roger into this."

"Impressive," I said as I wrote Penn's name down.

"Yeah, Roger and the senator were childhood friends," Mitchell said with a laugh. "It just goes to show it's not what you know but who you know."

"That's true," I agreed. "Is Roger the guy who got Cody the internship?"

Mitchell looked surprised again. "Wow. You really do your homework don't you? Yes, yes he is."

I decided to change track.

"Does Becky have any enemies?"

"No, she's a sweetheart. Everybody loves Becky."

With Leigh pulling for her and trying to help out, I figured that was probably true.

"How about Cody?"

Mitchell shook his head. "No, he was a good student and a great kid. Otherwise I wouldn't have asked Roger to try and help him get that internship."

"You really liked the kid?" I asked.

Sometimes the boyfriend will pretend to like a single mom's kids for the sake of, well . . .

"Like he was my own," Mitchell answered with a smile.

"Well, I guess that's all I've got," I said as I stood up. "I appreciate your help."

"No problem."

He stood up and walked me to the door.

"Let me know if you need anything else," he added.

I stepped outside.

"Oh, one more thing," I said as I turned back. "What do you think happened?"

Mitchell stood there, holding the storm door with his body.

"I don't really know."

"Do you think maybe Becky had a bad trip and killed her son while she was hallucinating?"

He stood there and thought about it for a moment.

"I guess anything is possible."

"Thank you," I said as I turned and left.

Interesting.

SEVEN

I left Jones's townhouse not knowing much more than when I'd gotten there.

One thing I had learned was that Becky wasn't used to shooting up heroin, at least when Mitchell was around.

Could she have accidentally overdosed? Could she have murdered her son in some type of delusional high?

I didn't think so. Like theatrical hypnotism, a subject would never do anything that they normally wouldn't.

But the fact that Becky's clothes were covered in Cody's blood didn't bode well for her.

A couple of things bothered me about her boyfriend. For a guy who went up to Camden Yards a lot to watch the Orioles play, why did he wait until almost halfway through the season to buy an Orioles program?

It was strange that he had a nice new program and the ticket to the game just sitting out there on the hallway table. It was like he'd left his alibi out for all the world to see.

But what bothered me the most was that when I asked him if he thought Becky had killed her son, he didn't say no.

Rather than standing up for his girlfriend, he threw her under the bus by implying that anything was possible.

Did he know something I didn't? Or did he want suspicion pointed at Becky?

When I got home I fired up the grill and pulled out a couple of hamburger patties from the freezer.

After I grilled them up, I grabbed a bag of Utz potato chips and brought my dinner along with a bottle of water into the living room.

I turned the television on.

I'd been watching the 1990 hit movie, *Pretty Woman.* I'd rented it from Blockbuster.

I pressed play on the remote.

Richard Gear had just carried Julia Roberts over to the piano and the two of them started making out.

As they kissed on screen, I diverted my eyes. It was awkward. I looked around my living room and time seemed to stop.

At that moment, my whole life seemed empty.

I could see that now.

I grabbed the remote and turned everything off. I sat there in silence and ate my dinner.

I had not allowed myself the pleasures of a woman for a very long time. Not since that day in Vietnam when I killed the little baby.

I guess it was my way of atonement for the innocent life I'd taken. I didn't deserve happiness or pleasure because he'd never have any.

As the years passed, however, I decided I would allow myself that happiness when I eventually found my life partner. I'd felt that Leigh could've been that person. But by the time we'd met, she'd already found her future husband. And since then, she'd had three kids.

I tried to look on the bright side. Being alone made you a dangerous operative. That's because you didn't have anything to lose.

You didn't care if you lived or died.

I knew for a fact I wouldn't want to run into someone like me in a dark alley.

I went to bed that night, dreading I'd have *my* dream again.

I wasn't disappointed.

After a restless night, I woke up early and did my normal morning workout.

I had two avenues of investigation ahead of me. One was to interview Roger Penn and verify Mitchell's alibi.

The second was to find some friends of Cody Whitfield and see if he'd gotten involved with some people he shouldn't have.

He was too young to have any real enemies. On the other hand, young men were disproportionately responsible for violent crimes.

Testosterone can be a bitch.

Before I started out, I called my good friend, Joe Wilson.

He answered on the second ring.

"Detective Wilson."

"Hey Joe, it's Gary."

"Well, hello my hardboiled P.I. friend. Is this a social or business call?"

I had to laugh. "Social," I said.

"Shoot."

"Bang!"

I couldn't help it.

"You and Carolyn want to go up to Blues Alley tonight? Eva Cassidy is performing."

I knew Joe loved Eva. We both did. We'd seen her last year. After the show, she was selling her first album, a bunch of duets with a musician named Chuck Brown. The record was titled, *The Other Side,* and Eva sold it on the street out of the trunk of her car.

Both Joe and I both bought a cassette tape.

"Carolyn's busy. She's going out with some friends, a girl's night out. But I can go."

"Great!" I responded. "I could use the distraction. You want the eight or the ten o'clock show?"

"Gary, I'm an old man with a *real* job. I can't keep up with a young whippersnapper like you! So eight."

Joe wasn't old. He was only 53. But I was glad to hear him joking around. After losing his son about a month ago, he'd been understandably down.

Truthfully, I was trying to get him out of the house as much for him as for me.

"Okay," I laughed. "I'll pick you up around six? We can eat there."

"Tell you what. I'll meet you at your place around six."

"Sounds good. See you then."

"Later."

I felt better having something to do that night. In the meantime, I showered, shaved, and put on a suit.

I looked at my reflection in the bedroom mirror as I straightened my tie.

I hated wearing a monkey suit. I was much more at home in military fatigues.

I hopped into my Corvette and took off for D.C.

Rush hour was nearing its end and I made it into the city in good time.

I found street parking, fed the meter, and then hoofed it over to the Capitol.

I've got to admit, I got a kick out of living in the suburbs of Washington D.C. I had major sports, theatre, museums, and great medical care at my disposal.

I was also just a couple of hours from the beach one way or the mountains the other.

But when I went into D.C., I couldn't help but be impressed walking around the most powerful city in the world.

I guess that's why almost every morning I ran around the National Mall.

And today, I got a thrill as I ran up the white stone steps of the United States Capitol!

I wanted to throw my hands up and dance like Rocky did in the movie. Instead, I just walked past the visitation desk and into the rotunda.

Once there, I looked up.

Beautiful!

I then asked a security guard for directions to Senator Frank Lindsey's office.

It didn't take long until I found it.

I walked through the open wooden doorway.

"Can I help you?" inquired a middle-aged woman dressed in a black pantsuit.

She was sitting at a desk facing the door.

"I was wondering if I could speak with Roger Penn."

"Do you have an appointment?" she asked, looking over at a calendar.

"Actually, no. I was just hoping I could grab a minute of his time."

"Well, he's in a meeting right now. If you don't mind waiting, I can find out if he'll see you."

"No problem," I said, as I took a seat on a brown wooden bench.

It was just like the military. Hurry up and wait!

But I knew he'd be busy. Besides overseeing the administration's office goals, policies, and procedures, he was in charge of the employees. That meant he was tasked with interviewing, hiring, training, assigning work, and writing performance evaluations.

I shook my head.

The fact I knew all that showed you maybe I'd lived in the D.C. area for too long!

There were a couple of other women working at desks in the large office.

Finally, a door from the rear opened up and four people walked out.

I stood expectantly.

"Mr. Penn," the woman with the black pantsuit said, turning. "This man would like to see you if you have a moment."

A man in a grey pinstripe suit looked over and appraised me.

"Certainly," he said. "We always have time for our constituents."

He confidently walked toward me and extended his hand.

Penn was fairly young. If I had to guess, despite his thinning hair, he was in his early thirties.

He wore black plastic-framed glasses that made him look like he'd walked right out of the 1950s. Penn had mousey-brown hair with flecks of grey. Despite a fancy tailored suit, it couldn't hide the fact he was developing a paunch around the middle.

He was followed by a young man who looked to be high school age.

"Gary Steel," I said as I extended my hand.

"Roger Penn."

He shook my hand with a practiced firm handshake.

"And this is our summer intern, Drew Harrison."

"Nice to meet you," I said.

"Hi," he said.

He was a good-looking kid. Sort of reminded me of Cody. Tall and lean with nice chiseled features.

I bet the girls like him.

I looked at Penn. "I have to admit that I'm not a voter from your state," I confessed.

"Oh?"

"Yes, I'm a private investigator and would like to ask you a couple of questions."

Seemingly, on cue, Ms. Pantsuit interrupted.

"Mr. Penn, don't forget you need to be in on a call in a couple of minutes."

"Thanks, Barb."

When Penn turned back toward me, I was ready to get the old brush off. Barb had set him up perfectly.

I could tell it was an efficient office. They pretended like they cared, but in truth, they really blew people off.

But who knows? Maybe they had to so they could get work done.

"Like she said," Penn started. "I've only got a couple of minutes. Let's step into my office. Drew, go grab a quick break and then see what you can do for Barb."

"Yes, sir."

You could have knocked me over with a feather, I was so shocked!

Maybe I was becoming too jaded in my old age?

I followed Penn into his small office. He gestured to a chair and closed the door as I took a seat.

I looked around. There were a lot of framed pictures of him shaking hands with famous politicians, including the president.

"So what can I do for you, Mr. Steel?" he asked as he sat down behind his wooden desk.

"I'm working an investigation. Can you tell me where you were last Saturday evening?"

He looked puzzled.

"Am I being investigated?"

"No. But if you could please just answer the question."

"Umm, I was up at Camden Yards to watch the Orioles."

"Were you alone?"

"No, I went with a friend."

"And his name?"

I could tell he didn't want to answer. I guess he didn't want to involve his friend in my investigation.

Reluctantly he answered, "Mitch Jones."

I nodded my head, letting him know he'd given me the right answer.

"And afterwards?"

"We went to a sports bar and had a few drinks."

"Where?"

"A place called Pickles Pub. Stupid name, but a good place."

"How late did you stay there?"

"Umm, until last call. Around 2?"

If that was true, it took about an hour to get down to Becky Whitfield's place.

Neither one of them had enough time to do the murder.

Penn looked at his watch. "Now if that's all, I've got to get on that call."

I stood. "Thank you for your time. I appreciate it."

"Certainly. I hoped I helped."

"You did. Take care."

I turned, opened the door, and left.

I made my way out of the Capitol.

Interesting. He never really wanted to know why I was asking. Maybe he already knew. Maybe he'd already talked to Mitchell Jones.

EIGHT

The next afternoon, Aisha Nader returned to Alexandria. Only this time she'd been instructed to go to the Chirilguas' main house.

It was a rundown place at the back of a dead-end street.

Javy Hernández had called her and told her to stop by that afternoon. They needed to talk.

Aisha had once again dressed down for the occasion. She still didn't feel safe around gang members and certainly wasn't going to do anything to advertise her femininity.

She wore baggy sweats with an oversize tee-shirt. She chose not to wear any makeup and her long black hair was pulled back into a ponytail.

Aisha parked her Escort next to a couple of beat-up old heaps at the end of the street.

As she got out of the car, she heard music coming from the house. The driving beat of the bass rattled the windows.

A couple of young men in jeans and tee-shirts sat lazily on the front porch. They were each smoking a cigarette and drinking beer. They watched her carefully as she approached.

Aisha could hear her heart start to pound in her ears as she walked towards them.

To her relief, they left her alone as she walked past them and through the open front door.

"*Chica!*" Javy said as he saw her enter the house.

He and three others were seated at a wooden spool that had once held telephone cable. It was turned sideways and being used as a table.

From the cards and coins on laying there, Aisha could tell they were playing penny ante poker.

Javy turned and yelled, "*Cortar la música!*"

The music was turned off.

"Good to see you again, *mamacita*!" he said as he stood up. "Let's go see *El Jeffe*!"

He walked over to her.

"And no stealing my money," Javy snapped, turning back at the others seated at the game. "I know how much I have!"

He led Aisha up stairs to the second story of the house.

Javy was silent as he led her down the hallway to a room.

They stepped into an old bedroom that had been made into an office.

El Jeffe, Angel Báez sat behind a battered desk. Across from him sat an enormous man.

Angel stood up. "Aisha, glad you could make it. Take a seat."

He motioned to where the big man sat. The man immediately stood up causing the wooden chair to creak in relief.

Holy crap! That's a big man!

Aisha took a seat once the big man was out of the way.

"This is Jose Lopez. We call him *El Intimidante,* The Intimidator. He'll be going along with you and Javy on our little mission."

Aisha looked up at the man and nodded. He looked down at her and grunted.

He was older than most of the men she'd seen in the gang, probably in his mid-thirties. The Intimidator was about 6' 8" and had to tip the scales at over three hundred pounds.

He certainly lives up to his name! she thought.

"So you found out where he lives?" Aisha asked, referring to Steel.

"Yes, he lives in Springfield. He does business out of his house. I've had a man on his place since this morning."

"When do you think we should do it?" Aisha asked, feeling excitement in her chest.

Angel paused and looked at his little army. "Tonight, you will strike! We'll teach this *gilipollas* not to mess with the *Chirilguas!*"

Javy clapped his hands together several times. "Yeah! And we're gonna get some revenge for my little bro, Fernando!"

"You still got your gun?" Angel asked Aisha.

"Yes, it's in my car."

"Perfect," Angel cooed. "My boys will be armed too. I'm afraid Mr. Steel is living his last day on this earth. He's gonna find out that crossing us is never a good idea!"

To this, the big man smiled and grunted. "This will be fun!"

Aisha looked up at him. "I'm glad you're on my side!"

The big man nodded.

"You will set out tonight at seven o'clock. Wait until dark to strike. Then carve him up leaving our calling card on his chest!"

The big man lifted his tee-shirt up and revealed a large hunting knife.

Excited, Aisha smiled at Angel. "Thank you for your help. I really appreciate it!"

"No problem. And maybe afterwards you can do something for me?"

"Sure," she said, smiling sweetly and batting her eyelashes.

Fat chance!

NINE

Death, taxes, and Joe Wilson being on time, those were the three things in life that I could depend on.

I don't know how he did it, but Joe was the most punctual guy I've ever met. If I didn't know him so well, I'd swear he'd park and hide around the corner until it was time to show up. He was that good!

Sure enough, at exactly six o'clock, my friend rolled up to the front of my house.

I stepped out my front door onto the stoop.

"Who's car?" I yelled as he got out.

"Yours. I'm low on gas. I could've filled up. But then I would've been late."

I laughed.

"We wouldn't want that to happen!"

Joe was just a whisker under 6 feet tall with silver-white hair. Like most middle-aged men he was fighting the battle of the bulge. Joe was coming straight from work which meant he was dressed in a dark suit with a skinny tie. He was also wearing a charcoal gray fedora. Think Joe Friday from *Dragnet*.

He started taking his coat, tie, and hat off and tossing them on his passenger's seat.

I went back inside, opened the garage, and took the Taurus wagon out. I hadn't driven it in a few days.

"Sure, take me out in the old people's car," Joe quipped good-naturedly as he slid into the passenger's seat.

"What can I say? I don't want you having a heart attack in my Corvette!"

Joe laughed and we were off.

It took a little bit longer than normal to get to Georgetown. There'd been an accident on I-395 and, even though it'd all been cleaned up, it still took a while for the backlog of traffic to clear.

I found paid parking at an all-night garage on Wisconsin Avenue, just down the street from the nightclub.

Joe and I walked the rest of the way.

Blue's Alley was an intimate, cozy club. It'd opened in 1965. Inside, it had about one hundred and twenty-five seats around small tables. As with most small clubs, seating was first come first serve.

But don't let the size fool you. Blues Alley has had some of the giants of Jazz come through its doors. Notable artists over the years include Ella Fitzgerald, Dizzy Gillespie, Tony Bennet, and Grover Washington, Jr.

Joe and I bought our tickets and went inside. There was a good-sized crowd for a Tuesday in the place already. We grabbed a table about halfway back.

We looked at the menus for a bit, and then a waiter came over. Joe ordered the Stanley Turrentine's Crab Cakes while I ordered the Maynard Ferguson's Cajun Chicken.

"And to drink?" the waiter asked.

I thought Joe would order a beer. But instead he said, "Water, please."

I realized that he was trying to drop a few pounds.

So, to support him, I asked for water too.

When the waiter left, I started to tell Joe about the case I was working on.

"You know she most likely did it in a drug-fueled rage," he said. "I've seen it before."

"Yeah, but her son?" I replied. "I don't have any kids—" I paused, briefly pantomiming, putting my thumbs underneath some imaginary suspenders. Then bragged, "—that I know of." I smiled and brought my hands back down. "But that just seems so unlikely to me."

Joe nodded his head. "That's true. But if not her, then who?"

"I need to talk to the kid's friends."

"Makes sense."

Our food came out.

I looked hungrily at my spicy chicken served over cheddar cheese grits and topped with mirepoix.

I looked over at Joe's crab cakes. His dinner was served with red beans and rice.

"Looks good!" I said.

Joe nodded his head. Then he bowed it. I knew he was saying a quick prayer.

I waited and then we dug in.

The waiter cleared our plates just as the show started.

Eva came out to a nice hand.

It was just a girl and her guitar. And with her talent that was all she needed!

I could tell at first she was a little stiff, probably a small dose of stage fright. And I couldn't say I blamed her.

But when she sang, brother! It was like hearing the voice of an angel!

She looked like one too. She was around thirty and when the spotlight hit her long blonde hair, it was like she had a halo around her head. She also had big, round beautiful eyes.

Eva sang all different types of songs: gospel, jazz, and blues. It was like she chose music that spoke to *her* and she wasn't about to get pigeonholed into any genre.

And when she sang her rendition of *Over the Rainbow*, I was reminded of the incredible power music has to move people. I'll admit it. I teared-up as she sang. Her voice washed over me and gave me chills. I couldn't help it. It was one of the most beautiful moments of my life.

If there's a heaven, this is what it's like.

After the show, we stood in line. Eva was doing a meet-and-greet and selling her cassette.

"Eva, you were wonderful tonight," Joe said as we got to the head of the line.

She looked at us, smiled, and looked down.

She was shy.

"Thank you guys for coming out to hear me," she said sweetly.

"You were great," I said as we shook hands. "I mean that. You are amazing."

I looked in the box next to her and realized she was selling the same tape she had last year.

"We'll each take one," I said and, turning to Joe, I stressed, "and I'm paying."

He'd already paid for dinner.

I reached into my wallet and pulled out a twenty.

She stopped and looked at us. "You two bought one from me last year, didn't you?"

"What can I say?" I smiled. "We love you."

"Thank you," she said as she handed us each a cassette tape.

"We'd love it if you'd put out a solo album," Joe said.

She blushed. "I'm looking into it."

"Could we get you to sign the cassettes?" I asked.

"Sure," she answered cheerfully.

She pulled out a Sharpie and asked our names. Then she signed the tape box.

"Thank you," we said.

"You have a nice night," Joe continued.

"Take care," I added.

"Goodnight. Thank you."

Imagine that. This gifted woman was thanking us!

TEN

I drove us back to my house. With little traffic on the road, we made it there in good time.

I stopped in the driveway and hit the garage door opener as Joe climbed out.

"Thanks for driving, Gary," Joe said, leaning in through the open door.

"No problem. You have a good rest of your night. And tell your beautiful wife I said, 'Hi.'"

I lifted my eyebrows up and down in my best Groucho Marx manner.

Joe just looked at me.

I loved kidding him about how she was out of his league. In truth, they were a great couple and she was lucky to have a good man like Joe too.

"Oh, that'll just make her day!" he retorted sarcastically. Then, "Let me know if you need any help with your case."

"Thanks, Joe. I appreciate it."

Joe closed the door and went to his car.

Meanwhile I pulled into the garage.

I got out of the car and pushed a button on the wall to close the garage door. Then, I went inside my house.

I went up the stairs and into the kitchen.

I opened the refrigerator looking for a snack when suddenly, the doorbell rang.

It wasn't my front doorbell, but the one to my P.I. office.

Strange.

I hustled down the steps, turning on lights as I went.

The doorbell rang again.

"I'm coming," I called out.

Finally, I came into the reception area. I turned on the outside light and peered through the peephole.

I saw a young woman with long black hair standing outside. She was swaying back and forth and looking over her shoulder as if she was afraid of someone following her.

I unlocked the door.

"Can I help you?"

"Are you Gary Steel, the private investigator?"

"Yes."

"I need to talk to you. Can I come inside?"

"Sure," I answered as I stood aside and let her in.

Maybe I was too relaxed in the afterglow of a wonderful evening at Blues Alley, but what happened next happened so fast I didn't even realize what was going on until it was too late!

After the woman stepped inside, I started to close the door. But it was ripped out of my hand and it flung open.

I turned to see what was going on.

All I saw was a shadow and a blur as an object speed toward my face.

Crack!

My head exploded with fireworks and I staggered backwards from the force of the punch.

I tried to remain standing. But despite my best efforts, I folded to the floor like a cheap card table.

The ground was spinning underneath me like a carnival ride as two men rushed inside.

I tried to scramble away on all fours, but I got kicked in the ribs.

Gasping for air, I rolled over onto my back and looked up at my assailants.

They were both Hispanic. One, the guy who'd punched and kicked me, was as large as a mountain. The other looked small even though he was probably of average height. He was young and chubby. If he didn't do anything about that, he'd be a fat man by the time he hit thirty.

I got a brief glance of a skull and Chirilaguas tattooed on his bicep.

Suddenly everything made sense.

I'd busted a drug ring the previous year. It'd involved the Chirilaguas. They'd sworn revenge on me for messing with them.

And by revenge, they meant death.

It wasn't the first time I'd heard that. But usually it was just an idle threat.

I guess this time it wasn't!

As I lay on the ground trying to gather my senses, I knew I was in trouble!

My foot fired towards Big Boy's kneecap.

To my surprise he slid sideways with the dexterity of a ballerina.

"Freeze!" His voice rumbled in a threatening and heavily accented voice.

That's when I noticed he had a gun pointed at me. In fact, they all had guns pointed at me.

My momma didn't raise a fool. I froze.

"Get up!" the Big Boy barked.

I stood up.

"Have a seat," he said, motioning his hand.

I slowly went around and sat down behind the receptionist's desk. It was a wooden antique that I'd picked up for its durability and looks.

"Now, *El Jefe* has instructed us to make an example out of you," Big Boy stated.

He smiled as he pulled a large hunting knife from the sheath that was looped to his belt.

"Yes, revenge for you screwing with my brother, you dumb fuck!"

I looked at the kid who'd spoken. He looked slightly familiar.

"Oh! I remember him," I said. "Good ol' fat Freddie. You look just like him. How is he doing in—"

I didn't finish the sentence. I was just trying to distract them by talking.

Striking as fast as I could, I reached underneath the old executive desk and hooked it with my arms.

In one motion, I stood up and threw the desk towards the men.

Gun fire rang out, shattering the silence of the night.

The desk hit both men forcefully and they fell backwards against the wall. As they slid down to the floor, I turned and started to run.

I bolted toward the woman. She was raising her gun.

I lowered my shoulder and hit her hard, like a pulling guard in football. She went flying backwards before she could get a shot off.

In a heartbeat, I was out of the reception area and flying up the stairs.

I heard a crashing noise.

"After him!" the man mountain yelled.

I didn't know if I'd been hit by a bullet or not. Adrenaline was pumping through me like water through a fire hose.

But I didn't think I'd been shot.

I took the stairs two at a time. The bottoms of my sneakers squealed like pigs as I thundered up the hardwood steps. Behind me, I heard what sounded like a stampeding herd of elephants.

I pivoted in the foyer and went up the last set of steps. When I got to the top of the stairs, I made a bee-line straight for my bedroom.

I flew into the room, reaching out and flipping the switch to the overhead light. I ran for the wall opposite my bed and pushed a hidden button.

A section of the wall slid open and I dove through.

I hit another button and the panel slid silently back into place.

I was safe for the moment.

I was in a small room that I liked to call 'The Pit'.

It was a secret room I'd built inside my house. Like the Batcave is to Batman, it was the nerve center of my detective agency. I kept important things in there, including documents, guns, high tech surveillance equipment, as well as other necessities.

It wasn't a very big room: six feet by twelve. The walls were lined with lead so that heat sensors from outside wouldn't be able to pick up my presence inside the house.

The lead also served to fireproof the room.

One of the walls had cool water trickling down from the top into a trough midway down. The water circulated in a continuous loop. It served as one way to keep the room cool. I needed the Pit cool to keep the equipment in tip-top shape.

Besides, I liked the sound of the water. It relaxed me.

I reached over to my gun wall and pulled two pistols from their holders. One was my favorite gun: a Walther PPK. I'm sure you've seen it before. It's the same type of gun that James Bond uses. I also grabbed one of my Glock 17s. They were both loaded and ready for action. I tucked the Glock into my waistband.

I heard a commotion outside in my bedroom.

"Where'd he go?" the younger man asked.

"I don't know," Big Boy responded. "Let's spread out and try to find him."

The female voice said, "I think we should get out of here!"

"Yeah, I agree with her," The younger man chimed in. "The dude probably has guns and he'll be coming after us."

I heard them rush out of the room.

I started up a wooden ladder that was attached to the wall. Near the top I stopped, reached up, and unhooked the latch.

I pushed up and opened the small hatch that led to the roof.

I climbed through the door. A muggy summer's night breeze gently caressed my face.

I started towards the front of the house.

They'll be leaving through the front door, I told myself.

That made sense. Why run all the way back down to the office door?

There were two possible exits that they knew of, but it wasn't really a 50-50 chance.

I stood at the edge of the roof, looking down into the darkness.

Sure enough I heard the front door open. Then I saw the storm door fly out.

From the inside ambient light, I could tell the girl was the first out. She was followed by the young kid, and then finally the big guy.

"Hey!" I yelled.

Big Boy stopped and looked up.

Perfect!

I stepped off the edge of the roof and, like a stone, plummeted down the eight feet or so towards his face.

Despite the shadows, he must've seen me coming because he tried to turn away. But it was too late! I managed to stick a landing squarely on his shoulder and the back of his neck.

With my two hundred and thirty-five pounds dropping like a rock, it must've been like getting hit by a freight train.

It was Big Boy's turn to crumple like a house of cards. I was glad to return the favor!

Like an expert surfer, I rode his body down the four steps that led to the cement landing below.

When he hit, I heard something crack.

Eww, that's not good.

I dove into a forward roll and landed on my feet.

I'd seen Big Boy lose his gun on the way down. I swooped over and grabbed it out of the garden. Then I turned and tossed it onto the roof.

I took a quick glance at Big Boy. He wasn't in very good shape. I didn't see his knife, so I left him moaning on the ground.

The girl and boy hadn't turned around to see what was happening. They were still running like scared rabbits straight for their car.

I heard the doors slam and the engine fire up.

As I ran towards them, the car started to pull away.

I immediately dropped to one knee.

With two arms outstretched to steady my gun, I tracked the moving car.

I squeezed the trigger.

The front tire blew out with a *pop!*

The car stopped moving. A split second later, it slowly started forward.

Tracking the car again, I took the back tire out.

Pop!

The driver continued to try and drive away. But not as fast as before. Because they were driving on wheel rims, they now had to fight the car's natural tendency to pull to the right.

Satisfied I'd slowed them down, I got up and sprinted after the car.

It was a small compact. I think it was a Ford, but to the detriment of me being a P.I., I was never very good at identifying the make and model of a car.

I could feel my muscles surge as I sprinted forward, all the while watching to see if the car doors would fly open.

But they didn't.

The car was tilting to the right. So I went to the other side and grabbed the car frame.

Keeping my head low, I shuffled along with the car.

I pulled the frame up, metal biting into my palm. I let the weight of the car drop. As it bounced, I pulled up on the car again.

This time the car bounced so high the tires almost came off the ground.

Not knowing what was happening, the driver stopped the car.

Even though it was dangerous, I had to risk it.

Do it!

I stood up, making my head an easy target for their guns.

This time, as the car bounced up, I lifted it up with all of my might.

I let out a loud *grunt* as I pushed the car up, finally rolling it over onto its side.

Then the sound of scraping metal, crunching glass, and shrieking people accompanied the movement of the car as it continued to roll, finally stopping upside-down.

The girl and guy hadn't used their seatbelts. Obviously, they were in too much of a hurry to get away.

Inside the car they'd tumbled around like laundry in a dryer.

It must have been the girl's car, because the guy was the one on the passenger's side.

Cautiously, I got down low on the ground. My hands could feel the cold hardness of the street. I looked inside the car.

The window's had shattered on impact and the upper part of the car was crushed.

Inside, the younger guy was trying to right himself.

He saw me and stopped.

"Hi," I said innocently after I'd noted that his hands were empty.

I reached in though the opening and grabbed the kid.

Then I literally dragged his ass out of the car.

"Stay!" I commanded. "I don't want to have to shoot you, Fat Boy. You'd be an easy target."

I figured he wouldn't move. I'd warned him in a way that had hopefully scared him. Also, from the bump on his head and the cuts on his arm, he looked to be hurt.

I ran back around to the other side of the car.

I had my gun out as I sneaked up on the girl.

In the dim light of the street light, I could tell that she was armed.

"Drop it!" I ordered from behind her.

She froze. I could almost see her thinking. If she turned, I would have to shoot.

"Don't!" I warned. "Or you're dead. I promise."

For years I'd been trying to learn to control my temper. On this night I felt like maybe—maybe—my bark was worse than my bite!

Reluctantly the girl tossed her gun through the window.

"Come on out."

I kicked her gun away.

By now I could hear sirens off in the distance. One of my neighbors had dialed 911.

Thank heavens!

I watched her carefully. She didn't appear to be as badly hurt as the boy.

"Okay, come on, get up," I said to her after she'd crawled out on all fours.

Slowly, she got to her feet. Earlier, I had just assumed she was Mexican because the two men were. But on closer examination I could tell she was of Middle-Eastern origin.

Revenge from the terrorists, too? How'd they ever meet up?

"Hey, Fat Boy, come over here!"

I heard some moaning and groaning, but he got up and gingerly waddled towards me.

"Let's go. Back to my house."

The three of us walked back together, slowly.

I quickly checked my hands. There were deep lines cutting across them. But the skin wasn't broken.

Thank heavens for calloused hands!

I quickly returned my attention to what was happening. I tried to squint through the darkness.

Where's Big Boy?

Then I spotted him. He was crawling into my neighbor's yard.

A moment later, a squad car pulled up, followed by another.

"Over here!" I yelled as a cop got out.

"This guy attacked us!" the girl yelled. "He's crazy! He's got a gun! Shoot him!"

"Hey Gary," said the first cop. "How's it going?"

The look on the girl's face was priceless! She wasn't going to be able to lie her way out of this.

"Oh, you know Barry. Same ol', same ol'."

The girl's mouth fell open like a drawbridge. I think you could've knocked her over with a feather.

The next car officer pulled up and a police officer got out.

"Hey Pete? How you doing?" I asked.

Officer Peter Sinclair was a veteran Fairfax County cop. And he was a good one!

"Seems to me I'm doing better than you are," he said, as he looked down the street at the upturned car.

Officer Barry King was cuffing my two captures.

"Pete, there's a big boy over there crawling into my neighbor's yard. He should be unarmed."

Pete looked at me and frowned.

"Thanks for the extra paperwork, Gary."

"Sorry about that," I responded. "I'll buy you a beer."

"You owe me a six-pack!"

He pulled his flashlight out and turned it on. He also pulled his gun.

"Well, back to work," he said.

A minute later he was back with Big Boy hopping on one foot while handcuffed.

It appeared he'd broken an ankle as well as other bones.

By now, people were coming out of their houses, looking to see what was going on.

A moment later, Joe pulled up.

He shot out of the car like a cannon.

He had his jacket and fedora back on.

"Everything all right?" he asked Officer Pete Sinclair.

Two more police cars pulled up right behind him, then an ambulance.

"Yes, sir," Pete answered. "Everything seems to be under control, although we don't yet know what's happened."

"Thank you, officer."

Joe walked over to me. "You all right?"

"I'm peachy," I responded.

I was on a one-man crusade to bring that antiquated word back.

"What are you doing here?" I asked.

"I heard a call on the police radio for a disturbance on your street. I knew it had to involve you."

"Really?" I asked.

"Yes. A disturbance? On your street? That's *so* Gary Steel!" he deadpanned.

I nodded my head.

"I guess so," I admitted.

"So what's this all about?"

"I'm not exactly sure," I said. "But let's go inside."

ELEVEN

Joe and I went inside while the EMTs examined the three would-be killers.

I took him up to the pit.

Joe was one of the few people in the world that knew about it.

Once he'd taken a seat, I started to tell him about what'd happened.

"I'm sure I captured most of it on my security tapes," I said as I hit 'stop' on one of the VCRs. Then I pressed play and rewind while turning on a monitor and hitting the 'source in' button.

We watched as the monitor showed things running backwards at a fast pace. Sort of like an old Keystone Cops movie in reverse.

When we got to where I wanted, I hit stop and then play.

The view was from an upper corner in my reception room and it was in crystal clear black and white.

I started to narrate.

"I heard my business doorbell ring and went downstairs to check out who it was. When I saw a female in distress, I opened the door."

I hit pause on the VCR as she entered the room and took a closer look at the TV screen.

"She appears to be in her late twenties, black hair, about 5'7" with a slender build."

I hit play.

"Then this happened."

Joe watched closely while I got sucker punched and, despite my best efforts to stay standing, crumpled to the floor.

He shook his head as I was quickly subdued by gun point.

"Pause," Joe directed.

I did.

"Why you?" he asked. "Do you know what this is about?"

"Notice the Chirilaguas tattoo here," I said, pointing on the screen to the smaller man's upper arm.

"From that drug bust from last year?" Joe asked.

"You guessed it! They wanted revenge."

"You were lucky, Gary. They could've fitted you for a pine coat right then and there."

Yes, my friend Joe Wilson sometimes talked like he was out of the 1950s.

"Yeah, but they wanted to make an example out of me. They wanted to carve me up. For some reason they wanted me alive while they did it."

"They wanted their pound of flesh before exacting their revenge."

"Yeah, you're probably right," I agreed. "Thankfully it bought me some time."

I hit play. On the monitor I got up off the floor and went around and sat behind the receptionist's desk. We watched as Big Man pulled his hunting knife out of the sheath.

"Ouch!" Joe said. "They were going to do more than carve you up!"

On screen, I started talking with Big Boy.

Joe leaned into the monitor and watched.

"This doesn't look good," he said, more to himself than me.

As soon as he said that, that's when I threw the desk at the two men and then darted towards the woman, knocking her over.

"Freeze it," he said.

I did.

"Rewind that."

I did.

"Pause it!"

I hit the button again. The action froze as I started to lift the desk.

Joe turned towards me. "How much does that thing weigh?"

"What? The desk? I don't know. Around one hundred and eighty pounds? Probably closer to two hundred with the supplies in it."

"And you just tossed it like it was nothing!"

"Well, yeah. But, Joe, my life sort of depended on it. It's amazing what adrenaline will do for you."

Joe shook his head in disbelief. "I guess all that weight lifting you do paid off."

I had to chuckle. "Yeah, I guess it has."

Switching between different cameras angles on different VCRs, I showed Joe the rest of what'd happened.

Joe covered half his face with his hand when he saw me drop from the roof and land on top of Big Boy, riding him to the ground.

"I'll tell you, Gary, you're a crazy mother fucker!"

After that, we watched as I cleared Big Boy's gun by throwing it on the roof. Then I knelt down and shot the tires out of the car.

That's when I ran out of frame.

"I don't have the rest of the action on tape," I said. "It happened out of camera range. But I went over and flipped the car as they tried to get away."

"You flipped the car?" Joe repeated, astonished.

"Well, yeah, I had to stop them."

"What are you, the incredible Hulk?"

I laughed again. "I like to think I'm more of a combination of Tarzan and Sherlock Holmes."

"You wish!" Joe laughed.

"You guys showed up soon after that."

Joe nodded his head. "Give me the main tape. I'll take it in and enter it as evidence."

"Sure," I said. "Let me dub a copy real quick."

My system was set up nicely!

I dubbed a copy and handed the original to Joe.

"Wait a sec," I said. "Let me break the tab so it doesn't accidentally get recorded over."

I stuck my thumb nail underneath the little plastic overhang on the side of the cassette and pulled it out, breaking the tab.

"Here," I said as I tossed the tab into the trash.

"Thanks," he said, as together we headed outside.

By the time we got there, Officer Sinclair was the only person remaining.

"Can we release the crime scene, Joe?" he asked.

"Not yet. There's a gun up on the roof."

Pete looked up at the top of my house.

"Really?"

I laughed. "I'll get the ladder. You get your camera and evidence bag ready."

He still didn't look happy and I had a good idea as to why that was.

"Hey, Pete, there's a deck on the back. You'll only have to climb up one story."

He smiled. "Okay, cool. Thanks, Gary!"

Ten minutes later, Officer Sinclair drove away with Big Boy's gun and my video cassette. Then I walked Joe over to his car.

"Well, thanks for stopping by," I said, sticking my hand out. He shook it.

"No problem. Now if you could please stay out of trouble for the rest of the night. I'd like to get some sleep!"

"Well, I'll see what I can do about that," I said with a laugh.

Joe started to close his car door. Then he stopped.

"Be careful, Gary."

I nodded. "Will do."

"I'm going to have a patrol car check on your street periodically over the next few days."

"You don't have to do that," I replied.

"I know I don't *have* to."

Deep down I knew Joe was probably right. The Chirilaguas had failed this time. That didn't mean they wouldn't try again.

I needed to start paying better attention. I had to go back to SEAL mode.

I guess deep down, I'd always felt sort of invincible. After all, I'd served two terms in Vietnam, and even back home, I'd been shot at and threatened.

I'd always been fine.

But, I knew the reality was. Anyone can die.

But do I really care if I do, Gary?

I let the thought drop. Instead I watched Joe start up his car and leave.

I stood there and watched him go.

Then I turned and went back inside. I fixed up the reception area that had been torn up in the altercation with the Chirilaguas.

As I turned the desk right side up, I noticed two bullets lodged in the top.

Even though I had to throw some stuff away that night, I decided that'd I'd keep the desk, holes and all.

It was good luck.

And who couldn't use a little good luck?

After I cleaned up, I went upstairs to hit the hay. Before I did, I popped four Motrin into my mouth.

My head was killing me.

TWELVE

Percy Willow looked down at his morning edition of the *Washington Post*.

As usual, he'd been up since 5:30, eaten, and already read the *Wall Street Journal*.

Percy read four to five newspapers a morning. Unlike most people, he read the financial section first, not the sports page, comics, or horoscopes.

As usual, he'd driven to his glass box of an office building in the high-end Tyson's Corner section of Northern Virginia.

It was now a little past 8 A.M. The morning sun had cut a bright swath across his plush carpet, lighting up the room as if it were noon.

This was his favorite part of the day.

Percy sat behind his desk, smoking his second cigarette of the day. He was mentally getting prepared for a nine o'clock meeting in the boardroom.

That's when he saw a headline in the Metro Section of the *Post*. It read:

ATTEMPTED MURDER IN SPRINGFIELD

Percy reached out and stubbed his cigarette out in an ashtray. He punched his reading glasses up his nose and grabbed the section. He quickly started reading the article. Without realizing it, he tapped the top of his mahogany desk with the fingers of his right hand in anticipation.

By the time he was through reading, his mind was already thinking about his next victim.

Ever since he'd gotten away with the murder of Penny Lancaster back in 1986, he'd been trying to make his hobby more challenging.

In 1987, while in disguise, he'd strangled an older woman in the basement of an office building, knowing full well that the action was being recorded on closed-circuit TV.

As he'd squeezed the life out of his victim, he'd been fascinated to see how her eyes had bulged out. He'd also enjoyed the look of terror that shot through them when the woman realized that she was going to die.

Percy had gently laid her on the ground. He'd then turned, looked at the camera, smiled, and waved.

The euphoria he'd felt from that murder soon dissipated. Percy realized that without motive tying him to his two victims, he hadn't really accomplished anything challenging.

Of course I got away with murder. Anyone would have!

He decided he needed to do something risky.

Whenever a spouse dies, the other one automatically becomes the main suspect.

Percy decided he would kill his wife, Angela.

* * *

It was 1990 and they'd been married for twelve years. In the beginning, Percy had been very attracted to Angela. Why not? In his own words she was stacked, had a cute ass, and could suck the chrome off a tailpipe. But, he also believed in the old saying, "For every beautiful woman you see, there's a guy who's tired of fucking her."

And, well, Percy was tired of Angela.

He believed that marriage should be a series of renewable contracts. Say maybe every five or ten years.

Angela had given him a son. But now, at the ripe old age of 34, she was starting to show signs of the passage of time.

Woe betide a woman who ages and starts to sag!

Over the last half of their marriage, Percy had cheated on Angela with other, younger women. Angela was well aware of his proclivity as Percy didn't bother to try and hide it. She'd put up with his infidelity because, well, she'd become accustomed to the rich lifestyle he provided.

Also, because she didn't have a job, she felt trapped.

Of course, being a beautiful woman, she had options. It wouldn't be hard for Angela to find a lover too.

But despite her being alone a lot —they'd sent their son away to boarding school —she waited a couple of years before taking someone to her bed. One of the reasons for the delay was simple. Angela valued her marriage vows. In her mind she had promised to forsake all others.

She knew Percy was wrong for sleeping around and Angela didn't believe that two wrongs made a right.

Finally though, she couldn't resist the temptation. As cliché as it seems, she slept with the pool boy. He'd graduated from high school that spring and headed away to college in the fall.

But the pool boy was just what the doctor ordered. He made Angela feel young, alive, and most importantly, appreciated.

After her summer love affair, it didn't take Angela long to graduate to someone her own age. His name was Marco Flores and he was a good friend of Percy's.

Angela wasn't a vengeful woman. But she had to admit that she climaxed extra hard when she realized it was Percy's dear friend Marco on top of her, pumping away.

On the other hand, Percy didn't really care. As far as he was concerned, the more Angela got it from someone else, the less he'd have to do her.

To him sex was just a way to feel good. And as far as he was concerned, like good food, it made sense to try different things and savor every morsel.

After all, isn't variety the spice of life?

So, it didn't bother Percy that Marco was fucking his wife.

But he did decide to use him in plotting her murder.

Sorry about that, old pal!

Unbeknownst to Angela, Percy had security cameras set up throughout the house.

That's how he knew the pool boy was screwing his wife, again and again and again.

Oh, to be eighteen!

Originally he'd decided not to confront her about her infidelity. And it paid off. She probably would have stopped if he'd broached the topic. Instead, the day he saw Marco in bed with his wife, he felt a visceral excitement.

How has this happened?

Percy traveled a lot. He also worked late a fair amount too.

This gave Angela's lovers plenty of time.

How can I turn this to my advantage?

Angela and Marco tended to stay in. Percy appreciated that. He didn't want people seeing his wife out on the town with another man.

Percy's customized setup enabled him to watch recordings of the security tapes in his office. Or if he preferred, he could watch it live online.

He'd paid for the best technology on the market and he used it.

Marco tended to come over to the house around noon.

A little afternoon delight!

Angela would greet him at the front door in something sexy, a glass of vino for him in hand.

They'd drink the wine and then go into the guest bedroom and go at it like a couple of rabbits in heat.

After a sweaty session that typically lasted about forty minutes, they stagger into the kitchen and eat lunch.

They usually had sandwiches.

Percy saw them do it so much that everything became predictable.

That's good. How can I use their predictability to my advantage?

One day, he watched Marco cutting their sandwiches with a long kitchen knife.

Perfect!

That night, when Percy got home, he took the knife, stuck it into a plastic storage bag, and hid it down in the basement.

After lunch, the lovers would sometimes go back upstairs and do it again. Other times they'd just take a nap. But regardless of what they did, they always drank more wine.

Then, after Marco left, Angela would clean everything up and make the bed.

Percy took his time and started plotting his D-Day.

Death-Day.

It was a Wednesday in July. That morning, Percy took the first flight out of Washington's National Airport and flew into New York City's JFK on a commuter jet. He took a taxi and checked into the hotel where he was giving a presentation later that day.

Once in his room, he changed from his suit into a pair of Levis and a tee-shirt. He added a mustache, a long-haired wig, and a pair of aviator sunglasses.

As he looked into the mirror, he smiled. His own mother wouldn't have recognized him.

Percy slipped out of the hotel and went to LaGuardia Airport and took another commuter flight back down to D.C.

It was a little after 10 A.M. when he arrived. He took a cab from the airport to a shopping center near his house and hoofed it the last two miles home.

Angela's car was gone. Percy was counting on that. The beauty of his plan was that, if things didn't work out this time, he could always try it another day.

There was no need to force things.

As was her usual practice, Angela had gone out to her late morning yoga class.

That gave Percy time to sneak into the house.

Making sure he wasn't seen, he went around to the back of his house and went in through the basement.

He took his wig and moustache off. He then went around the house and took down the hidden cameras.

Percy wasn't stupid. He wasn't about to commit a murder and have it recorded.

Some of the cameras were concealed in vents. Others were in a teddy bear, a clock, and two in smoke detectors.

Once he'd take down or disabled the cameras, he waited.

He didn't have long to wait.

Angela came home about 11:30 and immediately hit the shower. Then, at noon, Marco slipped into the house.

When Percy knew the coast was clear, he went up to the main level. That way he could hear what was going on upstairs.

Of course he heard the sounds of sex. It was strange and slightly erotic. He'd seen Angela and Marco making love before. But this was his first time hearing them.

It was hot.

Finally the sounds stopped and Percy returned to the basement.

He heard the two of them come down into the kitchen. They started to eat, talk, and laugh.

Wow, they really do like each other.

Afterwards, he heard them go back upstairs to the bedroom.

Percy tiptoed back up to the main level and listened.

After another quick session, he could hear them talking.

Percy moved into the stairwell to listen.

"I wish I could see you tonight," Marco said. "But Avery has a game."

"It's all right," Angela answered. "I'm going out with Julie. We're going to grab something to eat and then go see *Ghost*."

"I hear that's a chick flick," Marco laughed.

"Yes, but it has Patrick Swayze in it. So I'll love it!"

Percy heard Marco laugh again.

"See you tomorrow, Ange."

"I can't wait."

Percy heard Marco start down the hallway toward the stairs.

He rushed downstairs to the basement and waited.

The front door closed.

Percy took off all his clothes and put on some old leather gloves.

He then went into a storage cabinet and pulled out the kitchen knife.

As he crept up the stairs, he felt his heart pounding. His nerves tingled. He loved it! He felt so alive!

Angela was lying in bed with her back to the door.

She's taking a nap.

He slipped silently into the room.

Her back was to him, the sheet around her waist.

Percy stood there for a moment watching her back rise and fall with each breath.

Time for your last one.

He struck fast and violently.

With one vicious jab the blade went through her back and into her heart.

He hadn't stabbed her like Norman Bates in *Psycho*. Instead he thrust the blade forward so it would match Marco's finger prints on the handle.

Percy had worn the heavy winter gloves on purpose. He was glad he had. Otherwise, his hand would have slid down onto the blade and he'd have cut himself.

Angela made a gasping sound. As she woke up, she struggled to pull the knife out.

Percy stood back and watched.

Angela started grunting painfully.

She sat up and turned towards him, blood flowing out of her mouth.

Angela saw her husband standing there, naked, watching.

Why?

He smiled and watched her die. Then he went and showered and got dressed.

Percy left the front door unlocked when he left.

He got back to New York City in plenty of time for his four o'clock presentation.

Later that afternoon, Julie came by to take Angela to dinner and a movie. When Angela didn't answer the door, she went inside and made the grisly discovery.

It took a while, but Marco was eventually arrested for Angela's murder. The police had looked closely at the distraught Percy. But they couldn't prove that his alibi wasn't true. That he wasn't in New York at the time.

It was the fact that Marco was present at the house, his prints were on a wine glass and, more importantly, on the murder weapon. It didn't help that his semen was inside of Angela, too.

All of this evidence led to his conviction.

It was hypothesized that it was some type of lover's quarrel, like Angela refusing to leave her husband that motivated Marco to kill her.

Marco Flores was sentenced to life.

* * *

Since the murder of his wife, Percy had laid low. He hadn't even dated.

Percy lit up another cigarette as he read the newspaper article about Steel.

A former Navy SEAL. That should be a challenge. After all, he just thwarted a murder attempt by three people!

Percy had held off randomly killing people. But the time seemed to be right for a comeback.

Gary Steel . . .

Percy stubbed out his cigarette, rose, and put on his suit jacket.

It was time for his nine o'clock meeting.

And as usual, he was going to kill it!

THIRTEEN

I enjoyed a good night's sleep that night. So much so that when my alarm went off, I reset it to grab another hour.

Consequently, I'd decided not to go into D.C. and run. Instead I opted to get my running done in the neighborhood.

Afterwards, I did a full workout in my gym downstairs.

When I was through, I sat there on my weight bench, leaning forward, elbows on knees. Breathing hard, sweat rolled off my face and splattered in pellets on the floor mat. The speakers to my CD player blared, *Pat Benatar, Best Shots*, a greatest hits album. Ironically the track playing was *Hell is for Children*.

I have to admit, as I sat there cooling down, after the attempt on my life the previous night, it felt good to be alive.

A sixteen year-old kid is dead. I've got work to do.

I wiped my face with a towel.

I then got up, showered, and made a hot breakfast: French toast and bacon.

I washed it down with a can of Mountain Dew.

Yes, I know. Eww, soda in the morning!

You see, I don't particularly like coffee and sometimes I have to get some caffeine. So I have a Mountain Dew or a Dr. Pepper. It was a bad habit I picked up in the military. My mom would shoot me if she knew.

At nine o'clock I called the Fairfax County Adult Detention Center to check on Becky Whitfield.

I'm glad I made the call rather than just going down there. Like I'd suspected, she'd been arraigned and had already posted bail. She'd been released the previous night.

I called Leigh.

"Verizon, Ms. Ellerton, how can I assist you?" she answered, her voice sounding cheerful.

"Leigh? It's Gary."

"Gary, I was going to call you. Are you all right?"

"What? Yes. Why?"

I read about what happened to you last night in the *Washington Post*.

"Really?"

I was surprised. I had no idea. I didn't get the *Post* anymore. I'd been reading the *USA Today* for about ten years now. Truthfully it was for the Sports section. The *Washington Post* obviously concentrated on local sports and I was interested in the west coast scores too. So it was the late edition of the *USA Today* for me.

"Yes, I'm fine," I continued.

"I'm glad to hear that. It sounded awful. You could've died!"

"No. It was nothing."

I'm going to have to check that article out.

I thought of telling her that they shot up the desk I'd bought her when I still hoped she'd be my receptionist.

But this wasn't the time.

"I'm calling about Becky," I said.

"Becky got out! She's at a hotel."

"Hotel?"

"Yes, she didn't want to go home until the crime scene was cleaned up. She can't stay at her husband's place because he doesn't want her around the kids. And she can't go to my house. With our kids, George wouldn't stand for it. And even though I believe she's innocent, I can't say I blame him."

"Well, if you could tell me where she is, I'd like to talk to her about what Cody was up to that night. I want to talk to the friends that were with him."

"That's a good idea. She's staying at the Holiday Inn in Springfield."

"Good. She's not too far away."

In the background I heard a soft buzzing noise.

"Gary, I've got another call . . ."

"No problem. Thanks, Leigh. We'll talk later."

"Bye. Keep me informed."

And with a *click*, she was gone. I hung up.

I drove my Vet out of the garage. I must've really been zonked out the previous night because I noticed that the over-turned car was gone.

The police must've had it towed.

And I'd slept right through it.

I got on the parkway and headed up to main Springfield.

The Holiday Inn was a ten story structure near I-95. The building was one of the tallest in the area.

Springfield had been a bedroom community built in the 1950s in the suburbs of Washington D.C. The commute into the city had been an easy one until more and more housing developments had sprung up along Old Keene Mill Road.

Now, main Springfield was a hodgepodge of strip malls and buildings that, truthfully, was a bit unsightly.

Springfield, Virginia—the perfect example of urban sprawl.

I parked in the mostly empty hotel parking lot and made my way into the lobby.

I walked up to the front desk.

"Can I help you?" a friendly girl named Stephanie asked from behind the desk.

"Yes, I'm looking for Becky Whitfield."

"Just a minute."

Stephanie fiddled with a computer.

"Yes. She is here. I can't give you her room number. But I can tell her you are here."

"Sure, that sounds good."

She picked up the phone. I watched as she punched in 312. I could hear the phone ringing on the other end. On the second ring it was answered.

"Good morning, Ms. Whitfield. A gentleman is here to see you. A Mister . . ."

"Uh, Gary Steel."

"Gary Steel."

I heard Becky's voice responding.

"Okay. I will," said Stephanie.

She hung up.

"She said you can go on up. She's in room 312."

"Thank you," I said.

I took the elevator up and quickly found the room.

I knocked lightly.

I figured Becky might be high or drunk. It's what addicts do to cope.

But I was surprised. When she answered the door, she was dressed nicely, her hair was done, and she was wearing makeup.

She looked a lot younger than the first time I'd seen her. I guess the reality of her kid's death had sobered her up.

At least for now.

"Mr. Steel, come on in."

"Thanks. And please call me Gary."

I turned a chair around that was facing a desk and took a seat. Becky sat down on the unmade queen-sized bed.

"I'm looking into the night Cody died," I said, feeling a bit uncomfortable.

Becky nodded her head and I could see tears form in her eyes.

"I need to talk to his friends and find out what they were doing."

Becky nodded her head again. "He was out with his two friends, Randy Stevens and Robby Clarke. I'm not exactly sure what they were doing."

Becky started to blush when she realized she was admitting to not knowing what her sixteen-year-old son was doing that night.

She didn't need to be told that that wasn't good parenting.

"Can you give me the address of Randy or Rob?"

She stopped and thought for a moment.

"Umm, I don't know their address, but Randy lives at the corner of Queensberry Avenue and Ellet Road. Take a right on Ellet and it's just there on the right."

"Okay, Thank you, Becky."

She looked down at the floor.

"Are you okay?" I asked.

"I guess," she answered. "The best I can be. My husband won't let me see our kids or help plan my own son's funeral."

I didn't know what to say. So I just said, "I'm sorry."

I left Becky, still sitting on the bed and dabbing her eyes, with a promise that I'd let her know if I found out anything.

It was the second week of June. I knew that school wasn't getting out for summer for another couple of weeks. I'd have to bide my time to talk to the boys.

I went back home to wait things out. When I got there, there was a message on my answering machine.

"Gary."

I immediately recognized Joe's voice. "I just wanted to let you know that the girl from last night wasn't from the Chiri-laguas. From what we can gather, she's Muslim. I think she's connected to the Liberation Army's Fifth Battalion, from that terrorist attack you broke up last month. We're checking out her apartment now."

He paused, "Well, I guess that's it. Give me a call if you want."

I tried, but Joe was out.

I killed some time by running errands and going to the grocery store.

A few hours later, I pulled up in front of the Stevens' home.

The house was a split-level build, made of brick and aluminum sidings.

I parked on the curb, walked up the driveway, and then cut along the sidewalk to the front door.

I rang the doorbell.

A moment later a woman opened the door.

She was tall and lean with graying hair. She must've thought I was selling something because her face immediately looked like she'd smelled something bad.

She cracked open the storm door and looked at me expectantly.

"Mrs. Stevens?" I asked.

"Yes," she answered impatiently.

"I'm Gary Steel. I was wondering if I could possibly talk to your son, Randy?"

The momma bear in her immediately came out.

"What for?" she asked defiantly.

"I'm a private investigator." I handed her my Private Security Registration. It was what we had to use for a P.I. License. Unfortunately it was just a piece of thick paper with a computer printout on it.

No picture, nothing.

"I'd like to ask your boy about what happened on Saturday night with his friend Cody Whitfield."

She looked at the card skeptically. I could almost hear her thinking: *Anyone could print this out.*

I responded by saying, "Virginia DCJS (Department of Criminal Justice Services) is supposedly going to turn the licensing over to the DMV sometime soon. Then we'll finally get a real license with a picture on it. But for now, I know, it looks like some kid printed that off with a printing press."

She handed the card back to me.

"Well, whether this is real or not, I don't want you talking to my kid. He's pretty shook up and, to tell the truth, I think he's a bit scared."

"Ma'am, I understand you protecting your child. But Mrs. Whitfield has been arrested. I don't think a mother could ever do what they're saying she did to her child. I'm just trying to get to the truth."

I could tell my words chimed with her. She was probably thinking about the trauma that Becky had been through.

"Well . . ."

"You can call Fairfax County Police if you like. They can vouch for me."

"I'll do that. And if you are who you say you are, then I'll ask Randy if he's willing to talk to you."

She paused and looked at me.

"And if he says no, then that's final!"

"Sounds fair," I replied.

What else could I say?

She started to close the front door.

"Ask for Detective Joe Wilson," I managed to say before the door closed.

I stood out on the front stoop, brooding.

What will I do if he says no?

I would have no choice but to hope that the other kid, Robby Clarke, would talk to me. I might have to try and approach him away from his house.

I didn't like that. But I had to do what I had to do!

It seemed like I'd been loitering on the stoop for an hour. But it was only about five minutes.

Finally the door opened.

"Come in," Mrs. Stevens said as she opened the storm door.

"Thank you."

I followed her toward the back of the house and into the living room.

It was nicely decorated with comfortable furniture that looked well-worn.

A tall, lanky kid was seated on the sofa.

"Randy, this is Mr. Steel," his mother introduced.

Randy looked up at me. I stuck my hand out and he shook it.

I took a seat across from him in a matching chair.

"Thank you for seeing me," I said.

The kid looked pale and he had red rims around his eyes.

I guess I'd forgotten just how hard it was when a high school kid died.

Suddenly, I remembered what it was like to be in high school. I'd been in Texas and we'd lose one or two students a year to drunk-driving. It deeply affected the whole school, whether we knew the kids or not.

The loss of life, especially a young life, is tragic.

My brain briefly flashed back to Vietnam and the infant I'd killed.

I felt sick.

"I'm so sorry for your loss," I said sincerely as I came back to the present.

Randy nodded at me and I gathered my wits.

"Umm, so that night, what did you, Cody, and Rob do?"

I saw Randy's eyes shoot over to his mom and then back to me.

"Nothing special. We just hung out here for a bit and then we did some cruising around in the car."

"Okay," I said, nodding my head. "Did you guys get into any trouble with anyone? Someone who might have wanted to hurt Cody?"

"No!" Randy exclaimed. "No trouble. Everybody liked Cody!"

"Okay."

I had the feeling that something was going on. But Randy wasn't going to talk straight with me with his mother around.

I felt it was best I should let things lie.

"I appreciate you talking to me," I said.

I stood up.

"Here's my card," I said, stepping over to Randy. "If you can think of anything else . . ."

I handed it to him.

"And if you lose the card, I'm in the yellow pages under 'Steel Investigations'."

I said that last part in case momma bear took the card away from her son.

"Thanks for your time."

I gave Randy a slight nod.

I hope he understands.

Mrs. Stevens led me out.

"Thank you so much," I said. "I know that wasn't easy but I truly appreciate it. So does Mrs. Whitfield."

"Okay," she responded.

I could tell she wanted me out of the house.

I left.

I thought about trying to go see Robby Clarke. But I decided to give Randy the rest of the evening to see if he'd reach out to me.

With nothing else to do, I headed home.

FOURTEEN

I didn't have long to wait. I was sitting at the breakfast bar and eating leftover pizza when the phone rang.

I looked at my watch. It was 6:32 P.M.

"Steel Investigations," I answered, punching my business line.

"Can you meet me tonight?" a voice asked quietly on the other end.

"Sure, Randy," I answered. "When and where?"

"Lake Accotink. Under the train bridge. Around midnight?"

"See you then."

The phone *clicked* dead.

I pulled the handset away from my ear and looked at it.

Good job, Randy!

I finished my pizza and cleaned up. Then I went into the living room and finished reading the newspaper.

Around 8 o'clock, I turned on the TV.

Being summer, the schedule was dominated by repeats. Instead of watching *The Wonder Years*, I caught an *Unsolved Mysteries* that I hadn't seen before.

At nine, game one of the NBA Finals between the Chicago Bulls and the Phoenix Suns came on.

The Bulls with Michael Jordan, took control of the game early. Although in the third period, the Suns rallied and made it interesting. But in the end, it was the Bulls came through with a 100 —92 victory.

I listened to the last part of the game in my Taurus wagon as I headed to Lake Accotink.

I wanted to get there early.

The Fairfax County Park wasn't very far from my house and in less than fifteen minutes later I found myself pulling up to the access road.

I came to a stop when I saw a metal swing bar was blocking the road.

In the headlights I saw it was chained and padlocked shut.

I could've picked the lock. But instead, I decided to just park the car to the side. I grabbed my flashlight, went around the gate, and started jogging.

Glad I left early!

I snapped on the Surefire E2D Executive Defender flashlight. The high-intensity incandescent beam of light cut through the darkness like a hot knife through butter.

It was a police flashlight that Joe had turned me onto. It was made of black aluminum. It was small and had hard edges on each end that could be used as a weapon.

I loved the flashlight. Its only flaw was that it went through its lithium batteries pretty fast.

That's why I always kept spare batteries in both of my cars.

The access road was over a mile long.

I was making good time considering, I couldn't really open it up. The tree-lined road acted like a long, dark tunnel, blocking out any overhead light.

And despite the flashlight, I still had to be careful running because of the uneven pavement.

I chugged along at a steady pace. While doing so, I decided to practice running quietly, trying to not make any noise with my sneakers on the road.

"Always try to get better," I heard my dad's words echoing in my head.

The trees finally gave way to open space as I got nearer the train trestle.

I killed the flashlight and stuck it in the back pocket of my jeans.

The moon was shining overhead. It wasn't full, but rather a waning gibbous moon. I'd learned the phases in the Navy. It was the type of moon where you could see more than half of it illuminated and less than half of its shadow.

I was just grateful that I could move around now without a flashlight. I didn't want to advertise my presence.

Off in the distance I could hear the sound of water roaring like a standing ovation over the dam that was built at the south edge of the lake.

I kept running.

I looked up. The train trestle's shadow soared. If I had to guess, the bridge was about ninety feet high. It was longer than a football field. The bridge spanned the access road as well as the creek that flowed from the dam.

I'd been to the park several times over the years.

I knew that the original train trestle had been wooden and built in the 1850s. It was part of the Orange and Alexandria Railroad. During the Civil War, the bridge was targeted by Confederate soldiers. In December of 1862, Major Gen. J.E.B. Stuart sent twelve men to burn down the trestle. The bridge was quickly rebuilt and the Union continued to transport supplies along the line for the remainder of the war.

I checked my watch. The luminous dial glowed a ghostly 11:53.

I withdrew into the shadows by the road and waited.

Midnight came and went with no one in sight.

It was about seven minutes later when I saw movement coming up the hill from the lake. Two figures were walking down the road towards me.

They were quietly talking to each other.

Their voices carried well in the cool night air. But I couldn't tell what they were saying.

I didn't want to scare them. So as they approached the trestle, I stepped out of the shadows.

"Randy?" I asked quietly.

They stopped walking.

"Mr. Steel?"

"Yes."

We walked toward each other.

"This is my friend, Robby Clarke."

"Nice to meet you," I said, extending a hand.

We shook hands as he said, "Hi."

"So what's up?" I asked.

"Well, I wanted to tell you about that night without my mom around."

"I was hoping you would," I responded.

"Yeah, she took your card from me as soon as you left. I'm glad you told me you were in the Yellow Pages."

I smiled. I couldn't help it.

"Here, let's take a seat over here," I suggested.

I gestured to a picnic table.

We walked over and took our seats. Randy and Robby on one side, me on the other.

"Since it's a school night, I'm assuming you both snuck out of the house," I said in a soft voice.

The park was closed after dark and I didn't want to advertise the fact that we were there.

"Yes, we both live just a little ways north of the lake. We figured this was the safest place to meet."

"Yeah, we should get back soon," Robby said nervously, looking around.

"Well, let's get to it," I said. "Tell me about last Saturday night."

I figured they'd gone out partying. But I decided not to ask. It was their business. Besides, I didn't want to put them on the defensive.

I needed information.

"We just hung out at the lake," Randy replied. He looked at Robby for a moment and then continued talking. "We were smoking weed."

I raised my hand as I interrupted. "Do you guys owe for the pot?"

"No, we pay cash for it. Weed doesn't cost that much."

So much for a disgruntled dealer . . .

"Sorry," I said. "Go ahead."

"Usually, we all laugh and have a good time. But the more Cody smoked, the more agitated he got. We asked what was going on and he finally told us."

Randy stopped and I waited.

"He said he'd been forced to do some things he was ashamed of."

I leaned forward expectantly.

"He said during his internship he was forced to have sex with Senator Lindsay."

On the southern tip of Lake Accotink, Randy had just dropped a bombshell. The only sound was the rustling of water over the dam and the chirping of crickets.

"And you believe him?" I asked.

"He had no reason to lie," Robby answered. "He was totally bummed out."

"He'd decided he was going to tell his mom."

"But didn't he say he told Mr. Jones?" Robby asked Randy.

"Yeah, I think so," Randy responded. "To be honest, I can't remember everything. I was pretty high."

I wanted to tell them to steer clear of that shit. But I wasn't there to lecture. Besides, my words would most likely fall on deaf ears.

Instead, I asked, "Do you think he told anyone else?"

"No," Randy replied. "He said he told Mr. Jones and us and that he was going to tell his mom sometime over the weekend." He paused. "But not until she was sober."

"Cody said he'd tried to forget the whole thing," Robby added. "But he couldn't and it was driving him crazy."

"Yeah, he said he felt real guilty."

"What did Jones say to him?" I asked.

"He said he didn't believe it. But he'd look into it."

I had a bad feeling about this.

"And now someone's killed him," Randy said in a faltering voice. Through the dark I could feel Randy's eyes on me. "Do you think that's why he died? Someone's covering it up?"

"I don't know. But that's a heck of a motive."

We sat there in silence for a moment.

"Well, you guys should get home," I said. "Thanks for talking to me. It was brave."

They stood up.

"Yeah, I didn't like the idea of his mom getting arrested," Randy said. "She's a nice lady and I can't see her hurting him, ever. No matter what state she might be in."

"If you can think of anything else," I said, "you can always give me a call."

We shook hands and they started off, heading for home.

I turned and walked the other way on the access road.

I took my flashlight out and jogged back to the car.

My mind was racing.

A U.S. Senator? A cover up? That's *so* Washington D.C.

But killing a kid?

That's sick no matter how you slice it.

I hate people.

FIFTEEN

The next morning, I got a phone call from Leigh while I was working out.

"So what's happening?" she asked.

The night before I'd decided that I needed to play things close to the vest. It killed me. But for the time being I needed to keep Leigh in the dark.

My reasoning was simple enough. If I told her what Cody's friends had told me, she would tell Becky who in turn would talk to Mitchell Jones. Not that he was necessarily involved. But I wanted to approach him without the man being fore-warned.

After all, it looked like I was going to have to investigate him and the senator.

It seemed to me there was a good chance that Cody had told Jones and he'd told the senator.

Did Senator Lindsey have Cody murdered?

Anyway, that's why I'd decided to keep things quiet.

"Not much," I replied to Leigh. "But I'm still working on a couple of angles."

I hated myself for lying to her. But I also knew that I had to for her own good.

"Darn it."

I heard the disappointment in her voice.

"I'm sorry," I apologized.

Suddenly I didn't like the feeling that she might think I was an incompetent boob.

The call ended soon afterwards with me promising I'd let her know if I found out anything.

After the phone call, I cut my workout short and hit the shower.

I hurriedly got dressed and got into my Corvette. I drove straight to the Fairfax County Police Station on Rolling Road.

I went into the front desk. Someone was there I didn't know.

"Is Detective Wilson in?" I asked.

"Yes. Do you have an appointment?" the young man asked.

"No. But he'll see me."

"What's your name?"

"Gary Steel."

He picked up a phone and punched in three numbers.

"A Gary Steel to see you." He paused for a moment. "Yes, sir."

He hung up.

"You can head on back. Do you need me to show you?"

"I've got it. Thank you."

I headed back to Joe's office.

It was a glass cubicle and I could see him seated behind his desk.

It looked like he was doing one of his favorite things . . . Paperwork.

He saw me coming and waved me in.

"Sorry I'm interrupting you and your paperwork," I joked.

"I'd rather breathe bus fumes!" he complained.

I took a seat across from him. It was the first time I'd been in his office in a while.

He had a few family pictures on his desk. I noticed a new one. It was one of his son, Joey.

Joey had been murdered just last month and I felt a sudden sense of sadness wash over me.

He had been a great kid.

He was Joe's only son. He had two daughters left.

"How're you doing, Joe?" I asked.

He knew what I meant but didn't acknowledge it.

"Good, how are you doing?"

He didn't want to talk about it and I wasn't about to press the issue.

"I'm working on the Whitfield case," I said.

Joe looked at me quizzically. "I hear that's an open and shut case."

"Becky Whitfield didn't do it, Joe."

"Okay, but you've got to prove it."

"She doesn't have any motive for murder. But I know someone who does."

Joe lifted an eyebrow. "You do?"

"Yes. How about a U.S. Senator?"

"What?"

I had his full attention now.

"Cody Whitfield claimed that, while he was an intern, to have been coerced into having sex with Frank Lindsey."

Joe sat up in his chair and listened intently as I told him about my midnight meeting with Randy Stevens and Robby Clarke.

"Interesting," Joe said. "But you still have no proof. Not like the state has with Becky Whitfield's fingerprints on the murder weapon, as well as her blood soaked clothes."

"True that," I said, sitting back in my chair. "But I'm going to follow up on the lead and see what I can turn up."

"Be careful Gary. Fooling around with a U.S. Senator can be dangerous."

I smiled. "That's exactly the point."

Joe got the double meaning and let out a laugh.

"In the meantime Joe, if you can keep things quiet. I've got to figure out my next move."

"I've got no one to tell," he replied, throwing his hands up. "But let me know if you need help."

"Thanks."

"By the way, I was going to call you. The female who tried to kill you the other night? Her name is Aisha Nader."

"That name doesn't mean anything to me."

"She's not tied to the Chirilaguas gang."

"What? Then why was she there?"

"She has ties to Ramzi Sheikh Mohammed. In fact, we believe she's his girlfriend."

Suddenly, a frosty chill descended on the room.

Mohammed was the mastermind of the terrorist attack I'd thwarted just last month.

His girlfriend? I thought he was married. Well, I guess he was more American than Muslim.

"Seems like your enemies are coming together with a common cause," Joe said, looking pointedly at me. "To kill you. I think you should be careful, Gary. There might be another attempt and I've been to enough funerals lately to last me for quite a while!"

"Well, this stinks!" I eloquently replied.

I sat there for a moment and pondered what Joe had said.

He was right. I needed to be a bit more cautious!

I stood up. "Well, I'll let you get back to your paperwork."

"Just shoot me now!" Joe quipped.

I laughed and we shook hands.

"Hey, Joe," I said, getting serious, "I gotta get you back out running with me."

He'd quit running after Joey had died. I needed to get him back out for his health, as well as trying to get him back into the land of the living.

Joe nodded his head. "I will, Gary. Soon."

"Promise?"

"Promise."

That's all I could do. I nodded my head and left.

SIXTEEN

Percy Willow was sitting behind his desk, doing paperwork. He had a cigarette hanging from his lips and a short glass filled with Grand Marnier on the side.

The orange cognac liqueur was his favorite 'after work' drink.

It was indeed after hours and the office was empty.

The phone rang.

"Yes?"

The voice on the other end talked.

"Okay, send him up. And tell him to walk on back to my office. The doors are open."

Percy gathered up his papers and stuck them in his briefcase. He clicked it shut.

Off in the distance he heard the *ding* of the elevator.

He took his Grand Marnier and drained the glass like it was a shot.

Mmm, smooth.

He let out a little burp and stuck his cigarette back in his mouth.

A moment later a man walked into the office.

He was about six-feet tall, in his mid-forties, balding and had a little beer belly. He wore an open-collared white dress shirt, a blue sports jacket, and a pair of khakis with high polished brown loafers.

"Mr. Willow, I'm Benjamin Jet."

He stood there and waited for what came next.

Percy took it in and laughed.

Everybody did.

"*Benny and the Jets?* Like the Elton John song?"

Jet nodded his head and forced a smile. He was sick of it.

"I'm Mr. Harlow's investigator. He said you might need some help?"

Eugene Harlow was Percy's lawyer. He was a good one. Percy would have nothing but the best.

Gene Harlow and Benny Jets. Too funny! I guess you have to have a famous name to work there.

"Yeah, sure, take a seat," Percy instructed as he stubbed out his smoke.

Jet did.

"Do you know a private investigator by the name of Gary Steel?"

Jet sat there for a moment and thought about it. "No. But I think I may have heard the name somewhere before."

"Yes, he was in the newspaper just the other day. Some people tried to kill him."

"Oh yeah! I read about that in the *Post*. He seems like a lucky bastard. Err, pardon my language."

Percy laughed. "Don't worry about it."

Willow opened a drawer and pulled out an envelope. He tossed it onto his desk towards Jet.

"There's ten thousand dollars in there. I want to know every-thing there is to know about the man. His habits, his schedule, what he likes to eat, the color of his pee, who his friends are. Everything!"

Jet smiled and reached for the money. "I can do that. When do you want the report?"

"The sooner the better."

"Okay. Do you want the report delivered to you here?"

"Sure. Call me when you're done and we'll meet here after hours."

Jet stood up and slid the money inside his jacket pocket.

"Roger that."

"And Mr. Jet?"

"Yes?"

"No one knows. No one will ever know."

"Know what?" He smiled at his little joke. Then, "Understood."

SEVENTEEN

I was at a complete loss. I needed to figure this thing out—and fast! You can't just walk up to a U.S. Senator and say, "So I hear you've forced sex on an under aged boy?"

But maybe I could cause a panic and force him into a mistake?

I went to bed that night, running various ideas through my head. Finally, I decided to make my play. It was a weak one, but it was all I had.

I called Leigh the next morning and asked her to come by my office after work.

She agreed.

It was a little after six when she pulled up in front of my house.

I met her outside.

Leigh was dressed in a flowered dress with sandals. The dress hugged her curves and revealed a hint of cleavage. Her blonde hair was haloed by the late afternoon sun. I tried not to stare as it ruffled softly in the gentle evening breeze.

She tucked a lock of hair behind her ear.

Damn!

I felt my knees weaken.

Did I ever mention I liked her?

I was pleasantly surprised when Leigh walked up to me and gave me a hug. She usually didn't do that.

I gave her a polite hug in return leaning forward so as to not touch her boobs. I held her and patted her gently on the back.

"Come on in," I said nonchalantly, trying to be cool.

I gestured to the house.

She knows where it is, idiot!

We went upstairs and back to the sunroom.

"Do you want anything to drink?" I asked.

"No, thank you. I'm good."

She sat down at the breakfast bar on a stool. I leaned against the wall and watched as she crossed her shapely legs.

Damn! She's perfection.

"So, what's up?" she asked.

Stop staring!

"Umm, ah, first off," I eloquently started, "is Becky still staying at the Holiday Inn?"

"No, she moved back into her house today."

"Okay good."

Stop looking there. Look at her eyes!

"I talked to Cody's friends last night. The night he died he confessed that he'd been coerced into having sex with Senator Lindsey."

Leigh looked at me, dazed, as if I'd just struck her over the head.

"What? Nooo!"

The room was silent except for the sound of the air conditioner as Leigh contemplated my revelation.

"Oh, the poor kid!"

Her blue eyes welled up.

"Do you think Lindsey had him killed?"

"I don't know," I said. "Obviously, the senator wouldn't want it to get out. Cody had supposedly told Jones about being abused." I stopped. "I don't see anyone else who has the motive to kill Cody."

"What are you going to do?"

"I'm not really sure," I said. "But I do have an idea. It might tell us something or not."

"What?"

"Do you know if Jones is going to see Becky tonight?"

"I'm not sure. But it's Friday so I would think so. They're still in the hot and heavy part of the relationship. She tells me more than I want to hear sometimes."

"Okay. I'm going to need you to call Becky and tell her about Cody being abused."

"You haven't told her?"

"I have my reasons," I said, more defensively than I intended. "I want to get Jones's reaction to the news. If Becky didn't do it, she's being framed by somebody."

I stopped and let that sink in.

"Jones helped to get Cody the internship," I said. "He also bought the heroin that knocked Becky on her ass. I imagine he also has a key to her place."

Leigh's eyes widened. "I hadn't thought of that. Becky could be in danger!"

"I don't think so. She doesn't know anything. There's no reason to hurt her."

"Okay. But what are we going to do? Go to the police?"

"I already did. They're happy with their case and aren't going to look into it any further." I shook my head sadly. "I can't say I blame them."

Leigh looked at me. "Thank you for doing this, Gary."

I felt myself start to blush. So I changed the subject.

"I need to get Becky's address. I'm going to try and get into a position where I can spy on them inside the house. If I can observe them, I'll call you on my cell. I'll need you to call Becky and tell her that I've found a witness that claims the senator sexually abused Cody."

Leigh looked at me.

"I want to see how Jones reacts. I want to see if he immediately makes a phone call or something."

Leigh nodded her head. "That makes sense."

"If he's not involved, he won't do anything." I looked at Leigh. "I know, it's weak. But it's the only play I have at the moment. Will you help me?"

"Of course."

I smiled.

"I don't know her exact street address," Leigh started. "But her house is at the corner of Inverchapple Road and Hatteras Lane. Behind the house is a path to Lake Accotink."

"That's great," I said. "That helps a lot. I'll get the exact address from the phone book."

"If not, call me at home."

"I will. Thank you. And I'll call you if Jones shows up at the house and I can see them."

"She has a phone in the kitchen. It's in the back of the house. You should be able to get a clear view of it through the sliding glass doors."

I smiled. "That'd be perfect."

Leigh stood and we walked together to her car.

I stood on the sidewalk and waited for her to walk around to the driver's side.

Instead she stopped.

She looked up at me and hugged me. Then, to my shock, she kissed me on the cheek.

"I can't thank you enough."

Yes you can, I thought. Then, *Bad Gary! Stop thinking like that!*

"There's no need to," I managed to say.

I watched as Leigh got into the car. She started the engine up and drove away.

I stood there near the curb waving "goodbye" like a fool.

When she was out of sight I went back inside.

I pulled the White Pages out and got the Whitfield's street address: 5650 Inverchapple.

I jotted it down in a mini notebook.

I then went and made sure my 1992 Motorola International 3200 cellular phone was charged.

I loved the convenience of a cellular phone. I guess they're starting to call them cell phones now. But I swear they're almost the size of the walkie-talkies I used in the Navy.

I changed my clothes. I put on a black tee-shirt, black jeans, and black sneakers. I called it my burglar outfit.

If I was going to be sneaking around in somebody's yard, I needed to dress appropriately.

As the sky darkened, I went down to the garage and checked my supplies. I opened the back of the Taurus and grabbed my military-grade backpack. I unzipped it. I wanted to make sure that I had my binoculars. I did. I pulled them out.

Actually I kept a pair in both of my cars, as well as other stuff. I always wanted to be prepared.

I guess I would've made a pretty good boy scout!

I hopped in the car and put the binoculars on the passenger seat. I also put the mini notebook with the Whitfield address next to them.

I reached underneath the seat and pulled out a regional street map. It was actually a pretty thick book that detailed all the streets in Northern Virginia. You couldn't be a P.I. and not own one.

I looked at the first page of the book and found the area I wanted to see more detail of.

I turned to the page.

I knew where Inverchapple was. I ran my finger along it until I found the intersection with Hatteras Lane.

I'm glad I'd checked. The two roads actually intersected twice. But because I already had the street address, I would've ultimately figured it out.

As I backed out of the garage, I felt a twinge of excitement.

I loved working for myself. Don't get me wrong. I'd loved the military and following the strict chain of command. But I was older now and out in the civilian world. There was no "big picture" that I had to be concerned about. I was working for myself and not for some boss who was trying to profit from my own blood and sweat.

A few minutes later I found myself driving down Braddock Road. I took a right onto Inverchapple.

I cruised down the street, looking at the housing development. It looked like it had been built in the 1950s. The telephone poles held both phone and electric lines.

I started watching for the address.

There she is.

I pulled up to the stop sign that was right in front of Becky's house.

I grabbed a quick look. The house was small. At first I thought it was a rambler. But by looking at the surrounding houses I realized that it had a full lower level. From the front, it was below ground. But it was above ground in the back as the surrounding land sloped down away from the street.

Lights were on and two cars were present. One was parked in the carport and another one was parked right behind it in the driveway.

Good. Hopefully Jones is here with her.

I noted the back car. It was a light colored Honda Civic.

I couldn't get the license number in the dark. So I drove and made a right on Hatteras.

Like Leigh had said, there was a wooded area behind the house. I saw a Fairfax County Park Authority sign designating the pathway to the lake.

I drove past it and pulled up to the curb.

Other than a couple of houses across the street, the immediate area was deserted.

I reached up and killed the dome light in the car so that the interior wouldn't light up when I opened the door.

I looked around again.

A car came down the street and passed me by. Once it had passed the coast was clear.

I slipped out of the car and silently pushed the door closed.

I put the binoculars' strap around my neck and grabbed the cell phone. Then I started jogging down the path. Once I was deep into the woods, I turned and walked toward the house.

The lights were on in the back.

There was a deck on the back of the house and I was looking up at it from my current position. Unlike most decks, this one had solid walls on the sides. So I couldn't see through them.

I stepped out into the light as I walked closer to the building.

I stopped for a moment and considered going back to my car and getting camo-paint for my face.

But I decided against it.

I stepped back into the safety of the shadows.

I found a tree and did something I hadn't done in decades. I climbed it.

I didn't have to climb too high before I could see over the deck and into the house.

The double, sliding-glass doors gave me a good look into the kitchen.

I put the binoculars to my eyes. With lime green appliances and wooden brown cabinets, it looked like the kitchen had last been remodeled in the 1970s.

I saw two people seated around a small kitchen table drinking beer. It was Becky Whitfield and Mitchell Jones.

I assumed they'd just had sex.

He had his back to me and he was either naked or wearing a pair of briefs.

Becky wore a robe and it hung open with nothing underneath.

I guess I couldn't ask for anything better as far as observing them.

I dialed Leigh.

She answered on the second ring.

"Hello?"

"Now's the time," I said quietly into the phone.

"Okay," she said and hung up.

A moment later, I could hear the phone ring inside the house.

Becky stood up and closed her robe.

I couldn't hear her talking, but I watched through the binoculars. It was like I was standing next to her.

Pain and anguish washed over her face.

I watched as she talked to Leigh.

Finally, she hung up.

By now Michael was standing next to her; thankfully he was in a pair of boxers.

She explained everything to him and he hugged her.

As I watched her cry, I felt like a heel.

Couldn't I have found some better way to break the news?

But I needed to see Jones's reaction.

He was cool and calm as he comforted her.

Soon, they disappeared into another part of the house.

I stood on a limb and waited.

A few moments later I saw Jones again. He was dressed and he walked toward the front of the house.

He's leaving.

I thought about Becky. I hoped she was all right. First her son is murdered and then she finds out he was sexually abused.

Of course she's not all right, idiot!

I climbed down the tree and dropped to the ground.

I started running for my car when I heard a motor start up near the front of the house.

I got to my car as the headlights turned on and I quickly slipped inside. A moment later a silver Honda Civic drove past me.

It was Mitchell Jones!

I started my car's engine and watched as Jones took a left at the next intersection.

It was Queensberry Avenue.

I knew it hit Braddock Road in a mile or two. And from there it was a hop, skip, and a jump onto I-495, the Beltway.

Jones was flying through the residential area. I chased after him. Even with hitting fifty miles per-hour in the twenty-five mile an hour zone I was barely keeping pace with him.

And sure enough, up ahead, I saw him make a right onto Braddock Road.

I slammed the pedal to the floor and the car engine hungrily roared.

But he still had a big lead.

Thankfully, I was able to catch him at a light just before he got onto the Beltway.

A few miles later he took an exit onto I-395 north.

We were heading for D.C.

Is he going to see the senator?

EIGHTEEN

Of course not! I scolded myself.

Jones isn't friends with the senator: it's Penn who works for Lindsey.

As I sped after the Honda Civic, I decided it was a good time to run through what I knew.

I'd done it the previous night, but not in an orderly fashion.

Cody Whitfield had worked as an intern for Senator Frank Lindsey. According to his friends, Cody claimed to have been coerced into sex with the senator.

Cody got the job of intern through Roger Penn, Lindsey's Chief of Staff. Penn is best friends with Mitchell Jones, boyfriend of Cody's mom, Becky.

Mitchell had also bought the heroin that had incapacitated Becky during Cody's murder.

Besides his friends, Cody had also confided to Jones that he'd been sexually assaulted.

"And now I'm following Jones after he just found out that other people know about Cody's allegation," I muttered to myself.

I gripped the steering wheel tighter.

I'd been doing 70 in the 55 mph zone, and was once again falling behind Jones.

I jammed the gas pedal to the floor.

The car engine thundered causing the car to shake as it picked up speed.

I weaved through traffic like a drunken sailor in Chinatown

as I closed the gap.

On a straightaway, I glanced down at the speedometer. I was doing 85 and passing cars like they were standing still.

In case you were wondering, just because I have a private investigator's license, I wasn't allowed to break the law.

I could've been pulled over for speeding and everything would have been ruined. I would've gotten a ticket and lost Jones.

Fortunately, the police weren't around.

A minute later I was directly behind Jones's Civic.

I eased off the gas and I swear the car gasped a thank you.

Got to remember to get it into the shop for a tune-up!

Jones exited right and onto South Washington Boulevard.

I was about fifty yards behind.

After a bit, we entered the circle between the Memorial Bridge and Arlington National Cemetery. So far, this was exactly the route I took when I went into D.C. for my morning jog.

But instead of turning onto the bridge, Jones continued onto Arlington Boulevard.

A few turns and minutes later, we crossed the Key Bridge and entered Georgetown, not far from the Blues Alley where I'd seen Eva Cassidy just a few nights earlier.

But instead of heading toward the small concert hall, Jones drove north and into a posh residential area.

Because there weren't many cars out, I had to drop back and give Jones some distance.

You see, following a subject is a tricky proposition. You can't get on top of them because they'll know you're there. On the other hand, you can't give them so much room that you lose them.

I'd been tailing subjects for years and had gotten pretty good at it.

I was amazed that sometimes you could tail someone and they'd just have no idea that you were there. People who should've known better. People like the CIA or the Sheriff's department personnel.

I guess we can all get lost in our own little world!

At the moment I didn't realize how ironic that statement was.

Anyway, as good as I might be, I preferred using two cars on a surveillance. That way you could switch back and forth, taking turns at the initial tail of the subject.

Jones turned down a residential street. I didn't take the turn but instead slowly pulled into the intersection.

I killed my lights.

Luckily, I saw Jones park about halfway down the street. So I drove straight on and double-parked between two cars.

I left them enough room so that they could squeeze out if they needed to.

I got out of the car and ran down the street to where Jones had parked.

I got there just in time to see him get *buzzed* into the front of a small apartment building.

Drat! That's it. I've lost him.

Fortunately, there was no one else around on the quiet, exclusive lane. I slipped across to the other side of the street and watched the building. As I waited, I wrote down the apartment's number in my little notebook.

I figured it would match up with Roger Penn's address.

I gazed up at the building and felt helpless.

But luck was with me. A couple of minutes later I saw some

movement on the third floor.

Curtains were drawn back on the top corner apartment on the left side and two men stepped out onto a small balcony.

It was Jones and Penn!

I've got to get closer!

I hurriedly ran back across the street to the apartment building.

I thought of jumping up and pulling myself onto the second floor balcony, the one right underneath them. That way I could hear their conversation. But there was somebody inside that apartment and the risk of getting caught was too great.

That's when I noticed the corner of the apartment building. It had a decorative corner stone running up the sides. It had a small inch-wide lip in the stone about every twelve inches going up.

The groove ran the length of the corner stone, again about a foot long.

I reached up and grabbed ahold of one of the ledges with my fingertips. I put a toe on a lower lip and pulled myself up.

Carefully, I made like Spiderman and started climbing up the side of the building.

The dirty stone was coarse and ripped into my skin. It was hard keeping my 225 pounds from falling backwards.

But somehow I did it.

I climbed until my head was just above the bottom of the balcony they were standing on.

Now I could easily hear their conversation.

". . . so what are you going to do about it? Too many people already know!"

"Yeah, but they don't have any proof."

"Not good enough. The senator can't be the subject of rumor and innuendo."

They did it!

"Well, I put some fentanyl in Becky's heroin. When she shoots up tonight, she should O.D."

Becky!

"That was a great idea," Penn said enthusiastically. "I can see the headline now: **Grief-Stricken Mother Who Murdered Son Kills Herself**!"

"And it's a shame too. She's a good fuck. A middle-age woman who's getting divorced can get a little desperate . . ."

I didn't stick around any longer.

I climbed down a couple of feet and then dropped the rest of the way to the ground.

It wasn't the most graceful thing I'd ever done. I hit the ground and stumbled backwards over a bush. I landed on my butt in a side garden.

But I popped up like toast from a toaster and started running for the car.

I climbed in, found my keys, and turned the motor on.

As I started to drive, I grabbed my cell phone.

I called Leigh.

"Hello?"

It was George, her husband.

"Hey George," I said quickly. "Gary Steel, is Leigh there?"

"Yeah, sure."

I heard him call her name.

It seemed to take forever, but she got on the line.

"Hello?"

"Leigh," I said tersely. "It's Gary. I don't have Becky's

number with me. I need you to call her and tell her not to shoot up heroin. Jones has laced it with fentanyl. She'll die if she does."

"Okay, bye!" Leigh almost screamed into the phone.

"Leigh?" I yelled.

There was a delay and I thought I'd missed her.

"Yeah?" Leigh answered.

"Call 911 if she doesn't answer."

"Okay."

The line went dead.

By now I'd run a red light and was shooting over the Key Bridge.

It didn't take me long to get to the Whitfield's house because I sped the whole way.

I pulled up in front of the house. There was no ambulance. All was quiet.

This is either good or bad!

I parked in the driveway and got out of the car. I ran to the front door. I *banged* on it loudly.

I was too keyed up. I didn't wait for an answer.

I tried the knob. It turned.

Thank heavens!

In the distance I heard sirens.

Oh, crap!

"Becky!" I yelled. "Becky!"

No answer.

"Becky!"

I ran through the house.

I found Becky on her bed.

She wasn't moving!

NINETEEN

I'd seen overdose victims before when I was in Vietnam.

I knew that the body began to shut down as soon as ten minutes after shooting up. A heroin overdose slows body functions so significantly that there's a danger they might stop altogether.

That's when an overdose becomes fatal.

I noticed that Becky was still breathing. But it was shallow.

She was dressed in sweats and a UVA tee-shirt. Her hair was slightly damp.

She'd just taken a shower.

I pulled her eyelids back. Her pupils were pinpoint dots.

Grabbing her wrist I checked for a pulse. I guess I was pretty revved up because it was hard to find. But when I did, I noted that it was very weak.

As I put her hand back down, I noticed the skin was bluish around her fingernails.

Shit! She's shutting down!

"Stay with me, Becky," I said as I ran my hand across her forehead. "You're gonna make it."

I hope.

I slapped her face.

"Becky! Becky! Stay with me!"

She didn't respond.

I shook her.

Nothing.

"Come on Becky," I said, pulling her up.

I tried to stand her on her feet. But she was as limp as a rag doll.

"Come on, Becky, walk!"

Still nothing.

I laid her back down on the bed.

I need help!

I went outside to meet the ambulance. As I did, I left the front door open and I propped the storm door open by using the metal closer slide located on the closer cylinder.

Minutes seemed like hours. But finally the ambulance pulled up to the house with its siren blaring.

"A heroin-laced fentanyl overdose," I yelled as they got out of the ambulance.

The paramedic on the driver's side ran to the back of the vehicle and opened the double doors. He pulled out a large supply bag and started charging towards me.

"Take a right, last door on the left," I said as he ran past me.

Another man, the driver, quickly followed him in.

I stayed outside and started to pace. The coolness of the night air felt good. I hadn't realized I was sweating like a pig.

I took a deep, cleansing breath. It felt good to be alive.

I closed my eyes. *Come on, Becky!*

People started to come out of their houses to stare.

Some of the boldest started walking towards me.

I wasn't in the mood to explain to them what was going on, so I retreated into the safety of the house.

A couple of minutes later, someone came in the front door. I figured it was a neighbor and I was just about to lower the boom when I realized it was Leigh.

"How is she?" she asked.

It didn't take Sherlock Holmes to see she was upset.

"I'm not sure," I answered. "They're in there working on her. So I take that as a good sign."

Leigh hugged me. This time there was no politeness to it. It was a bear hug. I could feel her heart pounding through her chest.

"She's going to make it," I said positively, not knowing for sure if she would.

"If she dies it's my fault," Leigh said, tears welling up in her eyes.

"What? No!"

"I called her and got no answer. Then I dialed 911. But I didn't have her address. It took forever for me to find it! Those were precious minutes I wasted!"

"It's okay," I said softly. "She was still alive when they arrived."

Leigh looked at me. "Why are you dressed like a burglar?"

I laughed. I couldn't help it. I'd totally forgotten!

"I was dressed for work. Spying on people."

"How'd it go?" she asked.

Before I could answer, one of the medical technicians came back out.

He saw us and said, "Don't hold me to it, but I think she's going to make it. We've stabilized her and I'm getting the gurney. We're taking her to Fairfax Hospital."

"Need help?" I volunteered.

"I've got it."

In a flash, he was gone.

He came back into the house a minute later and pushed the gurney down the hallway.

I looked down at Leigh. She looked terrified.

"She'll be okay," I said hopefully.

Leigh nodded her head.

We stood there and a moment later the paramedics came back down the hall.

Leigh let out an audible gasp when she saw her friend roll by.

There was an oxygen mask over Becky's face and an IV attached to her arm.

Her color wasn't good.

"I'm going to follow them," she said.

"Okay."

I stood in the doorway and watched as everyone got into their vehicles.

And just like that they were gone.

I was alone in the house.

I was just about to turn off the lights and lock everything up when an idea hit me.

I wonder if Cody wrote anything down about his encounter with the senator?

I knew I was grasping at straws. But at the moment I had nothing else. So I closed the front door and locked it.

I couldn't have asked for a better situation: an empty house and the chance to search the boy's bedroom!

I walked back down the hallway, looking through the open doors.

The first bedroom had bunk beds and colorful stuffed animals in the room.

It was definitely a girl's bedroom.

The second room I checked out appeared to be what I was looking for.

I flicked the wall switch on and stepped into a boy's bedroom.

The small room had obviously been cleansed since the murder. The double bed was missing its mattress. Instead, all that remained was the box spring.

I imagine it'd been a bloody mess!

The bed had a headboard. It was the type that had shelves. On it was a clock radio along with two books. Both were by Stephen King, *The Stand* and *The Dark Tower III: The Waste Lands.*

At some point the clock had been unplugged. The time continuously flashed 12:00 A.M.

On the wall were posters. One was of the Washington Redskins celebrating their victory in Super Bowl XXVI. The other two were girly posters. One was of Cindy Crawford and the other was of Kathy Ireland.

Both of them were in bikinis.

As I *appraised* the Ireland poster, I realized that these were the type of posters you'd find at Spencer's, at Springfield Mall. They'd be in the back of the store near the black lights.

There was an old beaten up dresser in the room as well as a worn wooden desk and chair.

I pulled the seat out and sat down. The desk had a blotter on it that had doodles drawn all over it.

Cody had obviously gotten bored at times doing his home-work.

I looked around the room.

Where would I hide something in here?

I checked the desk drawer first.

It wasn't a particularly ingenious hiding place and I found nothing but pens, pencils, a ruler, a calculator, paper clips and other school supplies.

Underneath the drawer were shelves. I found notebook paper and some old school papers. I pulled them out. They had A's on them written in bright red ink.

I continued to dig through the junk.

I found a copy of the 1992-1993 edition of the Annandale High School yearbook.

There was other stuff crammed into the shelves. Things like a dirty white sock, football cards, and an old Butterfinger candy bar wrapper.

I stood up and went to the bed.

I grabbed the clock-radio.

Could he have snuck something inside?

No. The unit was solid.

I went to the dresser.

I started at the top drawer and worked my way down.

I didn't find anything until I got to the bottom drawer.

I lifted up a bunch of Levis jeans and found an old copy of *Playboy*. I pulled it out and opened it up. I found several other pictures stashed inside. They'd been cut out of *Penthouse* magazine and added to the boy's collection of girlie pictures.

I felt a wave of sadness wash over me.

He'll never know the love of a woman. Instead he knew the perverted attack of a lecherous old man!

I don't care what your sexual preference is. But nobody has the right to force themselves on anyone. Especially a child!

I felt anger start to burn inside me.

I wanted to hit something.

No. I wanted to destroy something.

Or someone!

I put the magazine away and sat back down at the desk, trying to calm myself.

I looked down at the floor and took a few deep, relieving breaths.

Finally, I settled down.

I've got a job to do.

I looked over at the closet. It had bi-fold doors and they were both pulled open.

Inside I could see clothes. On the shelves there were some boxes and old books.

I stood up and went over to look.

The books were old kid's mystery books that had probably once been proudly displayed on the headboard. Now they were stored on their sides in two columns. I imagine Cody felt he was too old for them.

When you're sixteen you want to grow up. Yet he hadn't thrown them away.

I recognized the light blue covers of the Hardy Boys. I looked closer and saw there were some Three Investigators books, and on top of one of the stacks was a Brains Benton mystery, *The Case of the Missing Message.*

I remembered that one from when I was a kid.

I had loved it.

A thought hit me.

He wouldn't, would he?

It seemed so apropos. The title sounded like a clue.

I reached up and grabbed the book.

I opened it. There was an inscription. It read:

To Becky!
Merry Christmas!
Love Mom and Dad.

It was his mom's book from her childhood.

I noticed in the back there was a piece of notebook paper. It was folded up.

Is it a bookmark?

I noticed there was writing on it.

Even though my heart started beating faster in anticipation, I told myself it was probably just a book report that Cody had done for school.

I remember doing that when I was a kid.

I have to admit, I was excited as I unfolded it. The first thing I noticed was that there wasn't a grade in red ink at the top of the page.

Instead, there was just some small, bold printing.

It cut deep into the paper as if the person who wrote it was agitated.

My eyes skimmed it like a rock skipping on a lake. My blood ran cold as I realized I'd found what I was looking for!

It was a letter written by Cody about being sexually assaulted.

I sat down at the desk and started to read it.

Dear God,

I'm writing this because I remember once hearing that it was good to write things down when you're upset.

Well, I'm more than upset. I'm angry!

I'm angry with you. I'm angry with the senator. I'm angry at the world. But mostly I'm angry at myself.

I don't want to be mad at you. Buy why? Why didn't you protect me? Why did you let this happen to me?

But I know deep down it's my fault.

I know better.

I shouldn't have been drinking. That made me weak. It also made it easy for the senator to take advantage of me. He told me by helping him get rid of stress I was actually helping my country.

Do you know how stupid that sounds when you're sober?!?

I love my country. I wanted to serve it.

But not anymore.

I hate Senator Frank Lindsey and all that he represents!

I now know the old saying is true. "Power corrupts. Absolute power corrupts absolutely!"

I hope they all go to hell!

What's hard is that something inside of me has changed. I am so ashamed I can't even look at myself in the mirror.

This would crush my mom if she knew. She's not exactly handling things very well at the moment.

I feel so alone!

God, I need your help!
Cody

I read the last few lines with blurry vision.

Tears had formed in my eyes and I felt sick for the boy.

I wished he'd talked to someone about what had happened to him. Then I realized he had.

Mitchell Jones!

I'm going to get him!

TWENTY

My due diligence had paid off. I hadn't really expected to find anything in Cody's room and certainly nothing like this!

I dug around in Cody's desk for some other samples of his handwriting.

I found one on a school paper. It was a report on *A Tale of Two Cities* by Charles Dickens.

'It was the best of times. It was the worst of times.' Indeed!

I turned the lights off in the house and closed things up.

I found a house key on a key ring in a bowl near the front door. I took it off and left it under the welcome mat.

I hoped Becky was doing all right. I would have to check in with Leigh in the morning.

I got into my Taurus and headed home.

On the way out of the housing development, I passed a car and noticed that it started up after I passed it. I felt like I'd seen it earlier in the evening.

But if they live around here, that wouldn't be unusual.

I continued on my way home.

It was late now and there weren't many cars out on the road. That made it easy to see if I was being tailed.

I was!

It had to be the Chirilaguas gang or the Liberation Army's Fifth Battalion terrorist group. And who knows? Maybe it was both.

They're back for another try, I thought.

I drove to my house and parked in the driveway. I left the headlights on and the car running.

I wanted the person to think I was going back out.

I went into my house through the garage door and then hustled through the weight room and out the back door.

I climbed the six-foot wooden fence and slipped through my neighbor's yard.

I'd noticed that the car following me had parked about one hundred yards down the street.

I crossed a street and cut through some other yards. Then I doubled back onto my street.

As I snuck up behind the running car, I saw there was just one person inside.

I ducked down and crept along the side of the car.

Then I stood up and flung the driver's side door open.

"Hey!" the man inside exclaimed.

I grabbed the guy by the collar and tried to pull him out of the car. But he had his seat belt on.

I quickly unclicked it and dragged his sorry ass out of the car.

I twirled like a dancer and threw him up against his car.

He tried reaching for the gun he had holstered on his chest. I delivered an uppercut to his gut and I could hear air explode out of his lungs. He fell to the ground on his side, the wind knocked out of him.

Maybe I was just in a foul mood, but after I bent down and relieved him of his gun, I reared back to kick him in the face.

"Nooo!" he wheezed as he threw his hands up.

I stopped short of using his face like a soccer ball.

"I give up! I give up!" he shrieked.

I reached down and, grabbing him by the collar of his shirt, yanked him off the ground.

I threw him roughly up against the car. And then, like that old fisherman joke, I grabbed him and did it again, just for the halibut.

I pinned him against the car and stuck my face in his.

I stared at him like a crazed maniac.

"I'm sorry. I'm sorry," he pleaded. "It was just a job."

The man was about six feet tall, mid-forties, and had a little gut.

"Tell your client not to fuck with me," I growled as I let go of his collar.

"Sure-sure," the man said as he bent over, hands on knees in obvious pain.

In the glow of the streetlight, he looked like he was going to throw up.

"Give me your wallet," I instructed. "I want to see your I.D."

Staying bent over and breathing loudly, he reached into his back pocket and handed me his brown leather, bi-fold wallet.

I opened it and saw his driver's license.

"Benjamin Jet of Washington D.C.," I said. I bent down next to him and whispered softly into his ear. "I'll remember the name. Benny and the Jets, right?"

I laughed at my little joke. Jet didn't.

Maybe he'd heard it before?

I put his wallet on top of his head.

That's it, I thought. *Make him look stupid.*

"I don't want to see you around here again," I snarled.

"No, problem," he said weakly as he reached up and took the wallet off of his head.

I could see he was starting to feel a little better.

I clapped him on the back. "As long as we understand each other, Benny."

I took the bullets out of his gun and pocketed them.

"I'll put your gun on the street corner over there," I said, pointing.

He nodded and I sprinted off.

I tossed the gun into the grass and continued onto my car.

I got in and pulled into the garage.

Looking back on it now, I realize that sometimes I get just a bit too stinking confident for my own good. I didn't push who'd sent Jet after me. I'd just *assumed* it was the El Salvadorian gang or the terrorist group.

And of course you know what they say about 'assuming'.

But at the moment, I was unknowingly the ass.

By the time I'd gotten into the house and peeked out of the window in my guest bedroom, Jet was pulling away after retrieving his gun.

The only thought on my mind was: *Well, that was fun.*

TWENTY-ONE

Percy Willow sat at his office desk the next morning. True to form, he was reading a newspaper and smoking a cigarette.

He'd received an early morning call from Benjamin Jet who'd wanted to see him right away.

Percy had told him to come on in.

The intercom buzzed on Willow's desk.

Rather than waiting to be told what it was about, Percy just hit the talk button and said, "Send him in."

"Yes, sir."

A moment later, Jet walked in.

He had a manila folder containing a typed-up report. He handed the file to Willow.

"I don't know what business you have with this Steel guy," Jet said as he sat down. "But I'd say stay away from him. He's one crazy motherfucker!" Realizing he'd just cussed, he quickly added, "Umm, pardon my French."

"What makes him a crazy motherfucker?" Willow asked, not batting an eye.

"Well, for one, he climbs up the side of buildings like the human fly! For another, he drives like a maniac. He drove 90 miles per hour after someone on the highway. And if that wasn't bad enough, he's violent! My guts still ache from where he belted me."

"He caught you?" Percy asked, sounding unhappy as he crushed his cigarette out.

"Yeah, he did," Jet replied defensively. "But not before I'd followed him for five hours from Springfield to Ravensworth to Georgetown back to Ravensworth and Springfield."

Jet pointed to the folder. "It's all in there. He was a busy bee yesterday, including being on the scene for an ambulance."

"But I told you I wanted to know his habits, his schedule."

Jet closed his eyes and sighed. "Gary Steel: born 1946 in Houston, Texas. A former Navy SEAL who did two tours in Vietnam. He spent twelve years total in the Navy. Afterwards, he went to Virginia Tech on the G.I. Bill. He kicked around for a few years doing odd jobs. Finally, he settled on becoming a licensed private investigator about eleven years ago. From all I could find out he's very good at his job. You may've read that he broke up a drug ring last year and a terrorist attack just last month."

Willow nodded his head. "I know."

"Well, his success has allowed him to pay off his house in Springfield."

Jet opened his eyes and looked at Willow.

"He owns a gun license and can legally carry a concealed weapon."

Percy nodded his head. His insides tingled with excitement.

Gary Steel seems like the perfect foe.

"Anything else?" Willow asked.

"Steel seems to have a soft spot for one Leigh Ellerton. They might be having an affair. She came to his house. When she left, they hugged and she kissed him on the cheek. Steel stood there on the curb, waving at her like a love struck puppy.

"I have a picture of them together in the file," Jet continued. "She works at Verizon. Ellerton is married with three kids. More details on her are in the report."

Jet reached into his jacket and pulled out an envelope.

It was the same one Percy had given him.

"One more thing," Jet said.

"Yeah?"

"He told me to tell you to not to fuck with him."

Willow's blood ran cold. "You told him I hired you?"

"No. He just said, 'Tell your client not to fuck with me'."

"So he doesn't know it was me who hired you?"

"Not from me."

Willow remembered the newspaper article that had brought Steel to his attention.

He doesn't know it's me. He must think it's the people who tried to kill him.

Jet tossed the envelope onto Willow's desk.

"That's about it. I quit. This guy's no dummy. He's dangerous and I don't want to mess with him."

Willow picked up the envelope and looked inside.

"I kept a thousand dollars for my troubles. It would've cost close to that anyway if I'd billed you my normal rate."

Jet stood up and turned to leave.

"Mr. Jet?"

"Yeah?" he said, turning back.

Willow tossed him the envelope. He'd thought about telling Jet to finish the job. But instead, Percy figured he might have enough information to go after Steel anyway.

"Keep it."

"Hey, thanks!"

"Now get out of here! I've got work to do."

Jet didn't have to be told twice. He tucked the money inside his sports jacket and hightailed it out of the office.

Percy watched Jet go. As the office door silently closed behind the private investigator, Willow wondered: *Maybe I should kill good old Benny first? Just for the hell of it . . .*

TWENTY-TWO

It'd been a long night. So the next morning, I decided to sleep in. But for some reason I couldn't sleep past 7:30.

Reluctantly, I got up.

It was too early to call Leigh to see how Becky was doing. But it wasn't too early to call someone else.

"Hey, Joe," I said after he'd answered the phone on the second ring. "Want to go running in D.C. with me?"

"Sure."

What? I was shocked. You could've knocked me over with a feather!

"Ahh, okay," I stammered trying to recover. "I'll see you in about fifteen minutes."

"Roger that."

I made a copy of Cody's letter and then carefully put it and his book report into a plastic Ziploc bag.

I brought it along with me when I climbed into the Corvette.

As I pulled up to Joe's house, he was already standing out front, waiting for me. He was dressed in dark shorts and a tee shirt, revealing a body that was as pale as a corpse.

It would be rude of me to comment on it wouldn't it?

"Quick! Get in!" I said as he opened the door. "Your neighbors are complaining about your white legs! They say the glare is so bright that they can't sleep!"

"Ha-ha," Joe responded as he sat down. "We all can't be bums and have a tan like you. I work for a living!"

"Hey! That's not nice," I responded in mock hurt as I gassed the Corvette.

I smiled broadly as in my peripheral vision I saw Joe's body fly back into the car seat.

The Vette squealed loudly, laying rubber on the pavement and kicking up black smoke.

"Maniac," Joe grumbled as he fastened his seatbelt.

"Speaking of working," I said. "I've got something for you on the Whitfield case."

"Yeah?" he responded suddenly interested.

"Yeah. Take a look inside the glove box."

Joe pulled out the Ziploc bag.

"Be careful. Just handle the papers on the edge. I'm trying to preserve the fingerprints."

"Well, look at you. A regular Sherlock Holmes!"

Joe cautiously pulled the papers out.

"A Tale of Two Cities?" he asked.

"That's a handwriting sample. Check out the other paper."

Joe switched pages and started reading.

"Holy cow!" he exclaimed.

Sometimes Joe talked like it was still the 1950s.

"This is the motive for killing the boy!" he continued. "I just wish Cody had gone into more detail about what'd happened."

I looked over at Joe.

"You want a child to describe his unwanted sexual episode with the senator?"

Joe was quiet for a moment.

"Well, yeah! I want to hammer this asshole's ass to the wall!"

I laughed. "I understand."

"Unfortunately, all I have is a 'he said - he said'. And one of the 'he saids' is dead!"

"I guess we've still got work to do," I said, stating the obvious.

I was pretty good at that.

For no apparent reason, Joe growled.

I guess that meant he agreed.

It was a Saturday morning and there wasn't much traffic on the road. Well, at least compared to weekdays.

We got to the National Mall in good time.

I parked on Constitution Avenue and locked the car.

We started our run.

It was a beautiful day in the Nation's Capital. The sun shone brightly and glistened off the reflecting pool. The marble of the Lincoln Memorial seemed to glow.

It'd been a while since Joe had gone running. So I slowed our normal pace down a bit.

And he kept up.

During the jog, I told Joe about how I'd overheard Mitchell Jones, Becky Whitfield's boyfriend, telling Roger Penn, Senator Lindsey's Chief of Staff, that he'd tried to kill Becky with a fentanyl-laced heroin drug overdose. I told Joe how the ambulance had taken her to the hospital and that I didn't know her current status. But I told him I still felt hopeful we'd gotten to her in time.

"I could lock her up for her own good," Joe said.

When I just looked at him he continued, "I'm a cop, damn-it. Heroin is a no-no!"

"No. Let's don't lock her up . . . yet."

When we finished our run, Joe bent over and put his hands on his knees. He was breathing hard and puffing like a runaway choo-choo train.

"You sadistic bastard!" he grumbled. "You just want to kill me!"

"Well, your wife is pretty," I responded. "And she's way out of your league!"

Joe threw a hand up in mock surrender. "No argument here!"

We'd wound up running at the Vietnam Memorial as usual. I went over and laid my hand on the etched names of a couple of buddies of mine who hadn't made it back home.

Joe respectfully stood back and let me have my time.

Then, together, we headed back to the car.

"So what's next?" I asked.

"I'm not exactly sure. I'm going to have to talk to the captain to see how he wants to proceed. This is going to be dicey. A U.S. senator having sex with an under age boy? Gee. Thanks Gary!"

"Glad to keep you busy," I deadpanned. "I wouldn't want you laying out in the sun and trying to get tanned legs!"

Joe ignored my joke.

"I probably should be asking you what you're going to do next."

Joe said it as if I were some troublesome child who was trying to ruin his life.

"First, I need to talk to Leigh and see how Becky is doing. Then I'm thinking of tracking down Senator Lindsey's current intern and talking to him. If I remember correctly, I met him when I went to see Penn."

"Sounds like a plan."

On the way home we stopped by Bob Evan's, a restaurant, and grabbed a hot breakfast.

Neither of us talked about the case. It was a nice little break.

I got home around ten o'clock. I picked up the phone and called Leigh.

"She's in stable condition," Leigh told me when I asked her how Becky was doing.

"That's great," I said, feeling relieved.

"I'm going to the hospital around noon to bring her home."

"You're a good lady."

"No, not really. It's what friends do."

"That's true," I agreed. "But she's got to do something about her habit or she's going to wind up dead."

"I talked her into going to rehab, even though things are a mess for her right now."

"That's great!"

"Yeah. But truthfully, Gary, I'll believe it when I see it."

"I know what you mean. She's got to want to change."

There was silence on the phone for a moment. Then I talked again. "Did you tell her about Jones overdosing her?"

"Yes. I don't want her to ever see that man again!"

I thought about telling her about Cody and the senator but decided against it. Even though it probably didn't matter anymore, I wanted to keep Leigh safe. And the less she knew the better.

All in due time.

"Tell Becky that I'm glad she's okay and that I'm following up on a lead."

"Really? What?"

"I'll tell you about it later."

"Okay."

"And Leigh, thanks for your help last night."

"No, Gary. Thank you for saving Becky's life."

"Oh!" I said suddenly remembering. "I locked up Becky's house. Since I'm pretty sure she doesn't have a house key, I left one under the welcome mat."

"Aww, that's great. Thank you, Gary!"

And with that, we hung up.

I sat there at the kitchen bar and thought. It was the weekend and the senator's office was closed. I couldn't remember the intern's name. So I guess I'd have to wait until Monday to follow up.

Unless . . .

I went downstairs into the gym and got in a good workout.

TWENTY-THREE

My initial impulse was to go straight to Roger Penn's Georgetown apartment, throw him up against the wall, and *politely* broach the matter with my fists.

But I realized I was being impulsive. More importantly, I was being stupid.

It was too early to show our cards.

I needed to get as much information as possible before the truth got blocked. Most importantly, I needed to get to the intern and talk to him about Lindsey.

So, for the weekend, I was going to have to do what I hated to do the most in the world. Heck, I imagine everyone hated doing it.

I was going to have to wait.

But it went with the job.

I decided to bide my time by going to the movies. One had just come out the previous Thursday that interested me. It was entitled, *Last Action Hero*. It looked like a kid adventure flick, but it had Arnold Schwarzenegger in it and I like his movies.

Besides, a good kid's story can be just as entertaining for adults too.

Sunday, I spent the day doing something I didn't usually do.

I read.

I pulled an old Stephen King book out of my bookcase. Seeing his books in Cody's nightstand reminded me I had one that I hadn't finished.

It was titled *Four Past Midnight*. It was a collection of four short stories. If they'd been written by anybody else, they would've been considered novellas if not full novels.

For dinner, I grilled a steak I'd gotten from Price Club and ate it out on the deck.

All in all, it was a pretty nice weekend.

Finally, Monday came.

Early that morning I ran in my neighborhood. Then I got in a good workout in my gym downstairs.

After that I'd showered, shaved, and headed into D.C.

When I got to the Capitol, this time I knew where I was going.

I took a seat on a wooden bench outside the office of the dishonorable Senator Lindsey.

There, I hurried up and waited.

It was just like being in the military all over again!

Around noon I saw the intern come out of the senator's office.

I was relieved to see he was alone.

The boy was wearing a suit off the rack. And why shouldn't he? He was probably growing two to three inches a year and there was no need to invest in a tailored one.

But right now, he looked awkward, sort of like a scarecrow in an oversized jacket.

"Hey," I said as I walked up to him. "I'm Gary Steel. We met last week."

"Oh, yes," he responded. "I remember. How're you doing?"

"Good, thanks. I forgot your name?"

"It's Drew, Drew Harrison."

"And you're Senator Lindsey's intern?"

"Yes."

"You mind if I buy you lunch? I'd love to find out about your job. I have a nephew who I think would love doing an internship here."

Dear reader you've just witnessed one of the key weapons of a private investigator. It's called, "pretense."

That's just a fancy word for 'lying your ass off'.

Drew took the bait.

"I don't have time for a sit down lunch. I was headed for the lunch truck that's just down the block."

"Perfect!" I said.

I got Drew two hotdogs, a soda, and chips.

I ordered a hotdog with mustard and a bottle of water to wash it all down with.

We grabbed a seat on a park bench and watched the sight-seers walking by.

It was an unusually comfortable day in the nation's capital. But I knew the normal summer humidity would rear its ugly head sooner rather than later.

I took a bite of hotdog.

"Mmm!" I moaned with my mouthful. "Boy, I tell you, a hotdog tastes so good outside, especially at a baseball game!"

"I agree," Drew responded. "They're tasty."

Well, so much for my world famous ice-breaking small talk. It was time to dive into the deep end.

"So what's it like working for the senator?"

I looked at him to see how he'd react.

"Oh, it's good."

I couldn't tell if he was hiding anything. But he didn't seem too enthusiastic.

I swam on.

"Do you get much one-on-one time with him?"

"No, not really. I tend to work in the main office. I run errands and make Xerox copies. Things like that. You know, normal entry-level stuff."

"The senator must work some long hours. Do you have to stay late?"

It seemed like I might have hit a nerve.

"I umm, sometimes," he stammered. "I try not to though. My parents don't like me out late at night."

I decided to change the subject.

"Where do you live?"

"Silver Spring."

That was a suburb of D.C. located in Maryland.

"I assume you take the Metro?"

"Yes."

I pulled a card out of my wallet. I was just about to hand it to him when on a whim I grabbed a pen and jotted Joe's information down underneath mine.

With the Chirilaguas gang and the Liberation Army's Fifth Battalion after me, there was no guarantee I'd be around to help the young man.

After all, anyone can kill anybody as long as they're willing to die too.

"Drew, I appreciate your input," I said as I handed him my card. "Here's my contact information in case you think of anything I might want to know."

"You're a private investigator?" he asked.

By the way his jaw dropped open like a drawbridge door, I could tell he was impressed.

"Yes."

At that moment I decided to level with the kid.

"Look, Drew, I've heard rumors that Senator Lindsey has been taking advantage of his interns."

Drew just looked at me.

"Remember. You don't have to do anything you don't want. Don't let anyone force you into anything."

He looked at me like he wanted to say something. But he didn't. Instead he ate a potato chip.

"I've added the contact information of a friend of mine. He's a cop. He's a good guy and would never let anything happen to you."

"Okay," Drew said suddenly standing up. "I've gotta go."

He tossed his trash and carried the rest of his food with him.

"Thanks for lunch," he said over his shoulder.

I sat there and watched him hurriedly walk away.

As I did, I couldn't help but get the sinking feeling that somehow I'd just blown the case.

I spent the rest of the day brooding and trying to figure out what I should do next.

TWENTY-FOUR

The next day was a normal Tuesday morning for Leigh Ellerton. At 6:05 her alarm would go off. She then went and showered. The reason she got up an hour earlier than necessary was so that her husband, George, wouldn't have to wait to use the bathroom. When she was through, he could just shower and then head onto his government job.

After Leigh was dressed and, as she liked to say, put on her face, she would wake George up. Then she'd go around and wake her three elementary school age children: Charlie, Ann, and Tommy.

Leigh would then head downstairs and make breakfast. Some days she'd make the kids a hot breakfast. It'd be something like waffles, French toast, or pancakes. At other times she'd just fix them up with cereal and milk.

While the kids ate, she would make lunches for those who were brown bagging it that day.

Today though was a good day. The cafeteria was having hamburgers with tater tots. That meant all of her children were buying.

So Leigh sat down at the kitchen table with her kids and enjoyed her morning coffee.

She had the radio turned on low to WMAL. She'd grown up with her mom listening to *Harden and Weaver*. And now, Leigh did the same. But last year Jackson Weaver had died. Frank Harden had continued with a show called *The Harden, Brant, and Parks Show.*

It wasn't the same though and Leigh was going to find another morning show to listen to.

Someday.

George came hurrying downstairs. He grabbed a glass of orange juice Leigh had poured for him and downed it.

He wasn't a big breakfast guy, especially since he was trying to drop a few pounds.

George Ellerton was in his forties with a receding hairline.

He was 5'9", which was average for an American male. But George supervised younger men and definitely felt like he was short.

He'd developed a middle-aged spread about ten years earlier. At one time it had been worse. But in the last couple of years he'd lost almost twenty pounds.

Even though George wanted to lose ten more, he'd had no luck in shifting it.

"Bye!" he said as he put the glass in the sink. "Everybody have a great day!"

He grabbed his briefcase, kissed Leigh on the cheek, and patted each of his kids on the head.

"Daddy's late!" he said.

"Daddy's always late," Leigh joked under her breath and the three kids laughed.

Then they echoed, "Daddy's late, daddy's late!" to gales of laughter.

George stopped and looked at his family with a pretend look of hurt. Then he broke into a big smile. "I'll get you for that," he said, pointing at Leigh. "Tonight, you're mine, babe!"

He winked at his wife.

Tommy yelled. "Ewww! Daddy's gonna kiss mom all over

her face."

More choruses of ewwws and laughter.

Leigh smiled and winked back at George.

And just like that, he was gone.

"Hurry up now," Leigh said. "The bus comes soon."

"I'm done!" Anna said.

"Go—"

"Brush my teeth," Ann finished the sentence, smiling, her big eyes beaming.

Leigh just shook her head. "Go."

Her children stood up and stampeded out of the room.

"Hey! Clear your bowls," she yelled after them.

But they didn't hear. They were too busy yelling at each other about who got to use the toothpaste first.

"Never mind. I'll do it," she said softly to herself.

Leigh smiled as she cleared the table.

She rinsed the glasses and bowls and thought: *I wouldn't trade my life for anything in the world!*

Leigh ushered the kids out the front door, making sure they all had their own backpacks.

"Charlie, you don't have to sit with them, but keep an eye on your brother and sister to make sure they're all right."

"Okay, mom, I will."

Leigh watched them run for the bus stop that was on the corner just two houses away.

Then she closed the front door and went upstairs to finish getting ready for work.

When she was satisfied with her makeup, Leigh put on the small black jacket that went with her black slacks and white blouse, an outfit she'd just recently bought at Macy's.

She kicked off her slippers and went to the closet.

Heels or flats?

Leigh chose flats. Unknowingly, a decision she'd be grateful for later.

She rotated side to side, checking out her image in the full-length mirror that hung behind the bedroom door.

Not bad.

Leigh was aware of her attractiveness to men. She tried to downplay her beauty and figure at work where she was fighting the never ending battle of female stereotypes.

On the other hand, she was proud of how she looked.

Not bad for three kids, she thought as she patted her tummy.

Part of her wished she could go back in time and redo her dating life. She loved George and would want to wind up with him. But it would be fun to go relive her youth and date with the confidence that she now owned.

Leigh believed she'd know who liked her for herself and who just wanted to get her into bed.

It was that latter fear that had held her up from dating very much.

She just didn't want to be a notch on somebody's belt.

Leigh slipped on her shoes. She was satisfied with how she looked.

Leigh thought of calling Becky but decided to get to work early and call from there.

It's always good to be seen arriving early.

She grabbed her purse and went to the garage. She pressed the button for the door to go up.

As Leigh walked around the car to the driver's side, she saw a figure enter the garage.

She couldn't describe the person because all she could see was a gun pointed at her.

"Hello, Leigh," the man said calmly. "Let's go back inside."

Stark, cold terror ran through Leigh's body like an electrical charge.

She thought for sure she was going to get raped.

Leigh decided she'd go along with whatever the man wanted, unless she saw an opening to get the upper hand.

Her first reaction was to not look at him. If she couldn't describe him, maybe he wouldn't kill her.

They were back in the kitchen now.

She was surprised when the man said, "Stop!"

She thought for sure they'd be headed for a bedroom.

Confused, she did as she was told.

"I want you to call your friend, Gary Steel," the man said. "I want you to ask him to come over. If you try to warn him or say anything funny, you *will* die."

The way he said it, she knew he meant it. But with Gary getting involved, Leigh realized she probably wasn't going to get attacked.

She turned and looked at the man.

He was tall, about 6' 1", with dark, grey-flecked hair. Although she didn't want to admit it, the clean shaven man was good-looking. He was dressed in a polo shirt, sports jacket, and slacks. The outfit showed off his athletic build.

His gun arm was extended toward her. She noticed that he was wearing latex gloves.

His other hand was tucked behind his back.

He looked at her with firm, dark eyes that showed he meant business.

Leigh fumbled for the wall phone.

She picked it up. "Umm, I don't know his number. I'll have to check my address book."

"Go ahead."

She pulled out a kitchen cabinet drawer and grabbed a tan book. It said, *Leigh's Friends* on the cover. George had gotten it for her when he was traveling on a business trip years ago.

She turned to "G" for Gary.

He wasn't listed under his last name.

With a shaky hand she dialed his number.

"Hello?"

Leigh started talking as she looked at the man.

She wanted to warn Gary, but she couldn't think of how. With a gun pointed at her, she could hardly think at all.

"Uh, Gary, this is Leigh, could you come on over?"

"Sure. What's up?"

"Umm, I just need you to come over. George is out of town and I need help moving something."

"Sure, I just got back from running. Let me grab a quick shower and I'll be right over."

"Okay. Umm, thanks, Gary. Bye."

Leigh hung the phone up.

"Very good," the man said. "Now, take a seat."

"What's this about?" Leigh asked.

The man walked behind her.

She smelled something sweet and then suddenly he put his hand over her face.

Leigh instantly started to panic and couldn't help but breathe in.

The man clamped the chloroform drenched rag tightly over

her face.

Slowly, she went limp and fell unconscious.

Leigh slumped down in her seat.

Percy Willow put the gun and rag down on the table. He reached into his coat pocket and pulled out a syringe. He injected its contents into Leigh's neck.

That'll knock her out for a long while.

He grabbed the rag and found a trash can and threw it away. Then, he washed his hands in the kitchen sink with the latex gloves on. He wanted to wash away the residue of the chloroform.

He found a dish towel and dried off his gloved hands. As he did, he looked over at Leigh.

That won't do.

He walked back around and pulled her up in the chair.

Suddenly an idea came to him.

Might as well distract him.

Willow unbuttoned Leigh's blouse halfway down the front.

Nice rack! Percy thought as he looked at her deep cleavage.

He pulled a breast out from her lacy white bra and left it exposed.

He stood back and looked at her milky-white skin and pale pink nipple.

Nice!

He reached out and squeezed her boob a few times.

He couldn't help it.

Real nice!

Then Percy grabbed his gun and went out into the living room to wait for Steel.

TWENTY-FIVE

I couldn't put my finger on it. But the phone call from Leigh seemed a bit weird. But hey, I certainly wasn't going to question it.

If she needed my help moving something, she'd have it!

I shower quickly. Then, looking at myself in the partially steamed mirror, I decided not to shave.

"Let's go for the rugged look," I said to my reflection.

I laughed.

"You're such a loser," I quipped as I threw on some Old Spice.

I put on jeans and an olive-green tee-shirt that was cut high in the sleeves showing off the muscles in my arms.

I debated between Nikes or combat boots.

I chose the sneakers.

Satisfied I looked the best I could for what I was working with, I headed down the steps two at a time. Then I hustled into the garage and got into my Corvette.

Corvette? Not shaving? Showing off the guns? How pathetic can I get?

Leigh lived about seven minutes away from me in Fairfax Station.

I made it there in five.

I pulled up to the curb and noticed that her garage door was open.

I headed for the garage and saw that Leigh's car was parked there and George's wasn't. I also noticed that the door to the house was open.

I stepped inside.

What I saw shocked me.

Leigh was sitting at the kitchen table. Her head was bowed as if she were in prayer. But what flabbergasted me was that one of her breasts was exposed.

"Leigh?" I yelled, suddenly concerned.

I started to run to her. But suddenly I felt a sharp pain tear into the side of my neck.

Historically, my fight or flight response has been to fight.

That's why I've told friends to never try and startle me. That is unless they wanted a fist thrown in their direction.

Upon feeling the pain, I instantly pivoted. My fist was already clenched and it started to fly toward the person standing behind me.

But instead of landing the blow, a blanket of darkness rushed over me like rain in a storm.

I felt myself start to buckle as the lights in my head went out.

TWENTY-SIX

Everything was going according to plan for Percy Willow.

He opened the other garage door and stepped outside.

Willow checked that the coast was clear. Then he hustled down the street to a white panel van he'd rented.

He drove it into the garage and once parked, pushed the buttons to close both garage doors.

Willow slid open the van's side door and pulled off his sports coat and tossed it onto the passenger side. Then he went inside for Steel.

Willow looked down at the man. Steel was a large, muscular man and Percy felt a bit intimidated. He saw that Steel's hair was still damp from a shower. Then he noted that Steel smelled good.

Yes, you like her don't you?

If he'd had any doubt before, Percy didn't anymore. He was definitely going to take Leigh along as insurance.

For what he had planned, a one-on-one against Steel might well be a losing proposition. And Percy couldn't have that!

He reached down and grabbed Steel by the wrists and started to pull. Willow struggled as he dragged Steel out into the garage and to the van.

I should take these stupid gloves off to get a better grip.

But Willow knew better. He hadn't been captured for his earlier murders because he didn't do stupid things.

"No clues left behind," was his motto.

From the rear, he grabbed Steel underneath the arms. He lifted and leaned back into the van, pulling the unconscious man along with him. Then Willow went around and pulled Gary's feet inside the vehicle.

Finally, he had Steel in the van.

Even though Leigh and Gary would most likely be knocked out for about a day, Willow grabbed some duct tape from his backpack and wound it around and around Steel's wrists and ankles.

He used a lot of tape.

Percy realized it was probably overkill. But after seeing the man in person and reading Jet's report on the ex-Navy SEAL, he knew he couldn't trust Steel as far as he could throw him.

And he knew he couldn't throw Gary Steel at all.

This guy could be formable! Maybe I should just shoot him now?

But Percy didn't. He was excited about his plan.

After Steel was secured, Willow went inside to get Leigh. Before he took her, he grabbed her boob and jammed it back into her bra.

But he decided to leave her shirt unbuttoned. He liked the view.

Leigh was much easier to get into the van than Steel. Percy just scooped her up in his arms and carried her.

After he got Leigh inside, he tied her up with duct tape too.

Satisfied they were both secured, he closed the van door and opened the garage door.

A minute later, he'd already pulled out and they were gone.

Percy drove the van to some land that he owned in Loudon County. It had a private air strip located off of Route 50. It was equipped with a small airplane hangar.

Inside the hangar, Willowed grabbed a portable conveyor belt and loaded the two unconscious people into his private jet.

Percy had gotten his pilot's license some twenty years earlier because he hated having to wait for the airlines. He had to travel a lot and he preferred to be in control of his schedule. So he'd gotten his pilot's license and then bought a Hawker 400: a small twin-jet corporate aircraft.

Once he'd done a final check of the airplane, he taxied out, and then took off down the small strip.

As the plane gained altitude, Percy looked around. It was a beautiful sunny day. The plane soared through the low clouds as he turned and guided it westward.

Willow felt a tingle of excitement. He realized he was going to do something that few people in the world had ever done. And it made him feel alive.

He glanced back at the two bodies lying unconscious on the floor and smiled.

Yes, Percy Willow was very excited.

TWENTY-SEVEN

George Ellerton left his job with the Federal Government every day at three in the afternoon so that he could be home by 3:20.

Deep down, Leigh Ellerton's husband felt blessed that he could get home from work and be there for his kids when they returned from school.

He'd make sure they'd have a snack, help them with their homework if they needed it, get them to any practices or ballgames, and figure out what to make for dinner.

Yes, George felt blessed.

He saw the school bus coming towards him down the street.

Perfect timing!

As he pulled into the driveway he noticed that his garage door was open.

Did I forget to close it when I went to work? George wondered. *But then Leigh would've closed it when she left.*

He wasn't worried as much as curious as to what'd happened.

He felt some relief when he pulled in and saw that his wife's car was parked in her spot.

She must have called in sick.

Leigh and George usually talked to each other once a day around lunchtime. That is, if they had a chance.

And the times they didn't talk, it wasn't a cause for alarm.

George got out of the car.

He walked into the house and called out, "Leigh?"

There was no answer.

Maybe she's napping.

George put his briefcase down on the kitchen table and ran up the stairs toward their bedroom.

But when he got there, the bed was made and Leigh wasn't in sight.

Where is she?

The doorbell rang.

Shoot! I forgot to unlock the front door.

He hustled down the steps to let the kids in.

You'd think they'd be smart enough to come in through the garage if the front door's locked.

George took a deep breath. He realized he was irritated.

Where is Leigh?

He opened the door and the kids came storming in like they were on the beaches of Normandy.

"Hi, Dad!" they chorused.

And just like that, the three kids were in the kitchen.

George was closing the front door when he noticed a car parked out front.

He hadn't noticed earlier. He'd been distracted by his garage door being open.

He walked out and looked at the car. It was a red Corvette.

He didn't recognize it.

Deep down, George Ellerton started to get a bad feeling. It was then that he decided to make some phone calls.

He called some of Leigh's neighbor friends. But no one had seen her.

Worried that he couldn't track Leigh down, he called her mom to see if she could come by and take the kids.

When she found out why, Leigh's mom became worried too. George had to promise he'd call her as soon as he got any word.

When the kids and his mother-in-law were finally gone, George called the police.

TWENTY-EIGHT

Buzz-buzz!

Joe Wilson looked down disapprovingly at the office phone on his desk. One of the buttons blinked a dull yellowish light.

Dammit! I just want to go home.

Joe was supposed to have clocked out about an hour earlier. But instead, he'd called his wife and told her he'd be late. He was sticking around the office to take care of some of the mounds of paperwork that'd piled up.

Well, no good deed goes unpunished . . .

He picked up the phone and punched the button.

"Detective Wilson," he grumbled as he sat back in his chair.

"Joe, it's Pete."

The caller didn't need to identify himself. Joe recognized Officer Pete Sinclair's voice right away. They'd been on the job together for what seemed like forever, and Pete was Joe's best friend on the force.

"What's up, Pete?"

"We got a call a few hours ago and I wanted to give you a heads up."

Joe waited patiently for Sinclair to continue.

"A man reported his wife missing. The officer on desk told him that since she was an adult and could come and go as she pleased, we couldn't do anything until she was missing for at least twenty-four hours."

Joe understood. He felt that not doing anything during the first twenty-four hours was stupid. But then again, how many adults really got kidnapped?

It would be a waste of the already stretched police manpower.

"Yeah?"

Joe was wondering why Pete was calling.

"Well, the guy said that there was an unidentified car parked out front of his house. So we sent a car out. The officer ran the plates."

Joe was starting to get a bad feeling.

"And?"

"The car belongs to Gary Steel."

"Give me the address," Joe spat as he sat forward.

Pete did and Joe jotted it down. He thanked his friend and hung up. He immediately called Gary. First, he tried Steel's residential number. When he got the answering machine, he hung up and tried the business number.

When he got no answer there, he called Gary's cell phone. Nothing.

Gary, where are you? Joe wondered.

He was concerned. After what'd happened the other night, his friend could be in big trouble.

He's a big boy. He can take care of himself. Joe swallowed. *I hope.*

Joe left a message on the cell phone. Then he stood up, grabbed his suit jacket and gray fedora from the coat rack and briskly walked out of his office.

Dressing as he walked toward the parking lot, Joe went straight to his car and took off.

Being a Fairfax County cop for as long as Wilson had, he knew his area pretty well. He recognized the street of the address he was headed to. He didn't need a map.

Joe was about ten minutes away.

He made it in seven.

When he pulled up in front of the house, he immediately recognized Steel's red Corvette.

Joe knocked on the front door. He had his credentials out.

The man who opened the door looked at Joe and then the creds.

"I'm Detective Joe Wilson. I'd like to ask you a few questions."

"Sure, come on in. I'm George Ellerton."

Joe stopped in the doorway. Ellerton was a unique last name.

"Are you Leigh's husband?"

"Well, yes. Do you know her?"

"Not exactly. My friend Gary Steel does."

They continued walking toward the living room.

"Gary?" George started. "I know him. Leigh's mentioned him before. He's a private investigator and right now he's helping out one of her friends."

"I'm familiar with the case," Joe replied. "That's his car parked out front."

"No! Have you talked to him? He might know where Leigh is!"

"Unfortunately he seems to be missing too."

Both men sat down in the living room. Joe sat in a chair that looked like a recliner. George took a seat on the sofa.

"You don't think . . . ?" George asked, suddenly distressed.

"No, Gary would never do that. He's as moral a guy as you'd ever meet. In fact he's a real boy scout!"

"Truthfully, I don't think Leigh would ever cheat on me either."

Both men sat there for a moment, contemplating things.

"Where do you think they are?" George asked.

Joe debated how much to tell Ellerton. He decided not to mention the attempt on Gary's life. After all, Joe didn't know if it had anything to do with what was going on.

So he ignored the question and decided it was best to start asking some of his own.

"When was the last time you saw your wife?"

"This morning, when I went to work."

Joe asked the normal questions. Does she have any enemies? Does she owe money? Does she have a drug problem?

The answer to all of these questions was 'no'.

Usually when a wife disappears, you suspect the husband. Joe's gut told him the man was sincere and didn't have anything to do with what was going on.

Besides, Steel was involved. He'd kidded Gary once that his middle name must be 'Trouble'.

They talked for a little while longer. But Joe felt like he wasn't making any headway.

He looked down at his watch. "I guess I'm through here. An officer will be around tomorrow to take an official report. In the meantime, if your wife shows up, give me a call."

Joe handed George his card.

"Day or night."

"Thank you."

"In the meantime, I'm going outside to check Gary's car for any clues."

"I'll go with you if that's okay."

"Sure. Just don't touch anything."

As they walked, Joe pulled out a pair of latex gloves from his suit pocket.

The car was open and the keys were on the floor mat in front of the driver's side.

"Obviously Gary wasn't planning to stay for long," Joe said as he held the keys up. "Even though this is a safe neighborhood, you don't leave your keys in a car like this."

Joe crawled further in and began to search the car.

He only spent about a minute looking.

"Nothing," he called out.

Joe got out of the car and locked it up. He stuffed the keys into a suit pocket. He'd turn them over to the officer who'd be investigating the scene the next day.

"Well, we'll be in touch," Joe said. "Remember, if anything happens, call me."

"Day or night," George parroted. "I will. And thank you for coming, detective."

They shook hands and then Joe got in his car and headed for Steel's house.

He pulled into the driveway. Joe had an extra key to Steel's place on his key ring.

He let himself in.

"Gary!" he called out as he entered the split foyer.

Nothing.

"Gary!" he called out again as he ran up the steps two at a time.

Joe didn't think he'd get an answer and he was right.

He went from room to room, looking for his friend. When he got to Gary's bedroom, he went to the wall and found the button to the pit.

He pushed it.

The panel slid open.

Nothing. No sign of Gary.

After Joe had cleared the upper level, he headed back downstairs.

"Gary," he called out again for no real reason.

He felt sick as he opened the garage door and flicked the light on. The Ford Taurus Wagon stood there, empty.

Joe looked at the downstairs bedroom and the weight room.

He stuck his head into Gary's empty reception area. Finally he went into Gary's office and sat down behind the desk.

"Where are you?" he muttered to himself.

He saw a blinking light on Gary's answering machine.

Without a thought, Joe reached out and hit the button.

"Tuesday, 10:32 A.M." the mechanical male voice of the machine said. Then: *"Hi, Mr. Steel, this is Drew Harrison. I need to talk to you. I'm afraid and I was wondering if you could come out to my house tonight around eight o'clock to talk. The address is . . ."*

Joe scrambled for a pen and paper. Fortunately Gary kept a small pad of paper and a pen right next to the phone for such an occasion.

"Don't call me back. Just show up. My folks will be gone for a bit so we can talk in private. Bye."

Joe looked at his watch. If he left now, he'd be able to make it up there in time.

TWENTY-NINE

When Joe got into his car, he radioed into the station and made a request. "I want the phone records for a George Ellerton—*Echo, Lima, Lima, Echo, Romeo, Tango, Oscar, November*—of Fairfax Station and Gary Steel—*Sierra, Tango, Echo, Echo, Lima*—of Springfield."

"Yes, sir. They should have them for you by noon tomorrow."

"I want them on my desk by 9:05 in the morning!"

"But, sir—"

"No ifs or buts!" Wilson whaled. "And speaking of butts, I'll have someone's if the reports aren't there!"

"Y-yes, sir."

"Out."

Joe hung up the radio.

Wilson caught a break because the traffic was light. Once he got up to Silver Spring, Maryland, he had enough time to grab a quick dinner. He went to a Burger King and ordered. Then he called his wife, Carolyn, from a pay phone to let her know what was going on.

He drove by the Harrison home, still about fifteen minutes early. Joe parked a little ways down the street in between two houses and finished his Double Whopper and fries.

The neighborhood was quiet. No one seemed to notice him. When it was time, Joe got out of the car and walked a couple of houses down and up the sidewalk to the house.

He rang the doorbell and pulled out his credentials.

A teenage boy opened the door. He seemed surprised.

"Can I help you?"

"Drew Harrison?"

"Yes."

"I'm Joe Wilson. Gary Steel sent me."

The tall, lean, good-looking kid blinked dumbly at the creds.

"Yeah, he gave me your phone number."

Joe exhaled. He'd been worried that the kid might not talk to him. But Gary had saved the day.

"Can I come in?"

"Sure."

Drew stood to the side, holding the door open as Joe stepped inside.

Joe took his hat off and took a quick look around.

The house had been built in the 1950s but Joe could tell that things like the kitchen had been updated.

The house was nice and quaint.

"We can sit here," Drew said, motioning to the living room.

Joe looked around. There was a high-end Sony Trinitron TV set on the entertainment center set against the wall. Wilson could tell that the furniture was high quality, probably Ethan Allen. A handcrafted leather sofa was book-ended by elegant mahogany end tables on either side. The tables matched the coffee table that was set in front of the couch. To the side, there was a leather chair. But Joe spotted a recliner and immediately sat down.

Joe was a recliner type of guy.

"Umm, I talked to Mr. Steel yesterday. He said he'd heard rumors about Senator Lindsey."

Joe nodded his head in understanding.

"I, well, umm, he also said I didn't need to do anything that I don't want to."

"Yes. That's right."

"Well, lately, the senator has been touching me."

Joe sat straight up.

"No. No, not that way," Drew stammered.

The boy's cheeks started to flush a bright red.

"Lately he's been rubbing my back. You know, sort of massaging me."

Joe nodded his head. He didn't want to speak. He didn't want the anger that would be in his voice to throw the kid off.

"This Friday we have an after work staff dinner in Georgetown and the senator really wants me to go."

Drew paused to gather his wits.

"After what Mr. Steel said, I'm worried."

"I'm glad you called," Joe said. "We'll figure this out."

THIRTY

I felt like I was at the bottom of a deep well. I groaned as I fought to wake up.

All of a sudden I felt a prick in my neck and blackness enveloped me once again.

I don't know how long I was out for, but once again I started to regain consciousness. This time I became aware that my head hurt and my body ached. I knew I was thirsty and hungry as hell.

I slowly opened my eyes and quickly realized I didn't know where I was.

As if in slow motion, I sat up. I saw Leigh lying not too far away from me on the ground.

I crawled over to her as quickly as I could.

"Leigh, Leigh," I said, panicking as I tried to feel for a pulse in her neck.

"She's all right," a voice said.

I turned and saw a man staring at me.

It was then that I realized I was in a basement. Fluorescent lights lit up the room. There were no windows in the concrete walls, just a heavy metal door that stood ajar behind the man who had spoken.

I noticed he had a gun in his hand.

"She'll regain consciousness soon," he said. The calmness in his voice was eerie. "Your metabolism, because of your muscular build, caused you to 'come to' more quickly than the average person."

"What's going on?" I demanded as I slowly stood up on wobbly legs.

"Settle down. All will be explained in due course. In the meantime, I have brought you something to eat and drink."

He pointed with his gun and I saw a pile of hamburgers, an unopened bag of chips, and a large pitcher of water along with two glasses filled with melting ice.

I also saw something that looked like duct tape on the ground.

He noticed me noticing.

"Yes, I tied you up with duct tape."

"What are you? Some type of hit man?" I asked.

He shook his head no.

The man was too far away for me to charge. Besides, I was still a bit woozy. I figured that if I could keep him talking for a while, it might buy me some time to gather my wits.

Then maybe I could attack!

"Are you working for the Chirilaguas or the Liberation Army's Fifth Battalion?" I asked defiantly.

The man tilted his head back and let out a hearty laugh.

He was enjoying this!

I quickly sized him up.

He was tall and lean. He appeared to be younger than I was, but not by much. He was wearing Army fatigues without any markings or insignias. He probably got them at an Army Surplus Store.

On his feet was a well-worn pair of combat boots.

In his tight fitting uniform, it was obvious that he worked out. He appeared to be in good physical health.

Well, except for the cigarette dangling from his mouth. He probably couldn't run worth a hoot!

"No, Mr. Steel," he said, "I am working on my own behalf."

He looked at me as he took a draw off his cigarette. He held it for a moment and then he released a puff of foggy gray smoke.

As he looked at me, he could tell I was confused.

"Have we met?" I asked as my mind whirled, trying to place the guy from somewhere in my past.

"No, never."

"But it was you who hired that P.I., Jet?"

He nodded his head.

Well, that took care of that piece of the puzzle.

Leigh groaned and I totally forgot about the man.

"Leigh," I said, kneeling down.

I softly brushed some hair out of her face.

Her eyes fluttered open.

"Gary?" she asked, confused.

"Shh. Take it easy. You've been drugged out."

She looked a little woozy. "What happened?"

"I'm not sure," I said gently. "We appear to have been taken captive and moved into a basement."

"It's not a basement," the man said testily. "It's an underground bunker."

Leigh heard the voice and I helped her sit up.

"Who are you?" she asked slowly, still in a daze.

"Oh, please, allow me to introduce myself. My name is Percy C. Willow and I am the man who is going to kill you."

I heard Leigh gasp as my blood ran cold.

I sat down next to Leigh and put my arm around her. I held her firmly as I tried to comfort her.

"Look, she's done nothing to you," I said, grasping at straws. "You want me."

Again with the hearty laugh.

Maybe I was wrong? Did he want Leigh?

"You've done nothing to me either, Mr. Steel," Willow said as he dropped his cigarette onto the cement floor and crushed it out with a boot.

I became aware that Leigh was buttoning her shirt.

Suddenly I remembered her hanging out of her bra.

I squinted angrily at the man.

Asshole!

I prayed that Leigh didn't know she'd suffered that indignity. She'd be humiliated if she did.

"Then why take us?" I asked.

"I want a challenge. No, I need a challenge. I read in the newspaper how you fought off three people trying to kill you. I figured you might be a worthy opponent."

"But why bring Leigh?"

"Because, for what I have in mind, I have to make sure you don't just run off. And think about it. A Navy SEAL versus an ordinary old businessman? It doesn't seem quite fair does it? But with Mrs. Ellerton on your team, well I figure that'll keep you around to play and even up the odds."

"Play? Play what?" I demanded.

That's when Percy C. Willow stood there and explained his sick plan.

"Over the last seven years I have murdered several people."

He paused to let the words sink in.

"It's sort of a hobby of mine," he said with a smile.

"What?" Leigh gasped.

I could feel her body tremble against mine and I pulled her in closer.

"You heard me," he said proudly. "I've killed people."

"Why?" Leigh asked.

"It's simple," he said coldly. "Because I can."

My skin began to crawl. If this guy was telling the truth, I didn't like it. It meant that he was confident that Leigh and I weren't going to live to tell the tale.

"So what're you going to do with us?" Leigh asked.

"Right now we are standing in my bomb shelter. Well, actually, it's my "rich people's" bomb compound. For safety's sake, we are hundreds of miles in the middle of nowhere. I have three structures, one above ground and two below. I have enough food and water, as well as an underground ventilation system, to house me and my family indefinitely in case of a nuclear attack.

"After you eat and drink," Willow continued, "you'll go out this door, and I will hunt you down."

This felt like some type of nightmare. Only I couldn't wake up.

He stopped and looked at us.

"Of course I'll give you a sporting thirty-minute head start."

"But that's insane!" Leigh wailed.

"On the contrary," Percy snapped. "It's quite sane."

"It's like that story, *The Most Dangerous Game*," I said.

Willow laughed. "Precisely!"

I'd read the short story back in school. But I didn't remember it. I just remembered that some type of big game hunter decided to hunt humans instead.

Life imitating art?

"And if we refuse?" I asked.

"Then I'll just have to gun you down where you stand."

By the tone of his voice and the look on his face, there was no doubt he meant it.

"But you can't kill her," I said, motioning to Leigh. She's a mother of three. I promise. I'll play your game."

"I don't give a rat's ass whether she's a mother of three. I can and will kill her!"

I looked over at Leigh. She looked terrified.

"It'll be okay," I said softly.

Willow looked at his watch. "I suggest you eat now. We shall begin within the hour."

With that he sat down on the ground, pulled out another cigarette, and lit up.

I helped Leigh over to the food, where we sat down on the floor.

I had no idea how long we'd been unconscious, but we were both starved. We began eating and drinking what could very well be our last meal.

"What are we going to do?" Leigh whispered as she leaned into me.

"I don't know," I said with my mouth full. "We'll have to assess the situation once we get outside."

THIRTY-ONE

At first, Leigh and I wolfed down the hamburgers like there was no tomorrow. Gradually though, we slowed down.

I think the food helped both of our heads to clear. At least I know it helped mine.

"Can we take the leftovers?" I asked.

There was an extra hamburger and a half a bag of potato chips left.

Willow flipped his hand into the air as if to say, "Whatever."

Leigh put the burger into the chip bag and rolled the top over and over a few times.

"You can get your canteens out front," Willow said. "They're filled with water."

He looked at his watch.

"It's about time to head out."

I looked at Leigh; she looked pale. I didn't need any great deductive powers to tell that she was terrified. I tried to give her a reassuring smile as I helped her to her feet. Then together, we started towards the door, walking slowly like a couple of condemned prisoners heading for their execution.

Willow stood back and watched me carefully as we passed by. Then we headed out the entrance.

I thought about trying to close the iron door. But seeing that there was a long tunnel up ahead, I didn't like our chances of getting away.

It'd be like shooting fish in a barrel.

Best to play it straight, I thought. *For now.*

Side-by side, Leigh and I walked up the slanting passageway. I protectively kept an arm around her shoulder.

At the end of the tunnel were two large doors. I pushed the bar on one of them as we walked out into the bright sunlight.

Cool air smacked me in the face.

Wearing just a tee-shirt I realized I was a bit under-dressed for the elements.

Through squinting eyes, I looked around.

I saw a nearby building that looked like a concrete barracks. It was long and one story high.

There were no cars around. In fact, to my shock, there were no roads. Just a nice-looking private jet and a small blacktop landing strip.

We were in a large clearing.

I didn't know what I was expecting, but my hopes started to sink.

Off in the distance, I could see mountains surrounding us. And I'm not talking about little east coast mountains. I quickly realized that we'd been taken out west. I was looking at the Rocky Mountains!

"Toto, I have a feeling we aren't in Virginia anymore," I quipped under my breath to Leigh.

"Yeah, I was just noticing that."

We stopped and I bent down and picked up two canteens. By their heft, I could tell they were full.

I then put their straps over my shoulder, one on each side.

"You've got half an hour staring right *now*!" Willow barked.

He was looking at his watch.

I looked at my wrist. No watch. I usually wore one. It was a nice Seiko I'd gotten on leave while in Hong Kong. But since I'd hurried to get to Leigh's house, I'd forgot to put it on.

"Come on," I said, turning left and heading into the woods.

Once we were out of sight, Leigh stopped and turned towards me.

"Just go on." She pleaded, looking at me. "I know that you can make it out of here without me. Then you can come back with the authorities and get the sick bastard!"

"I'm not going anywhere without you," I said firmly.

"But look at how I'm dressed? A pants suit and flats! I'm no good in the wild!"

"Doesn't matter," I said. "We're both alive and we're gonna both stay that way."

"But you're playing right into his hands. That's why he brought me."

"Leigh, we're not discussing this anymore. It's you and me, together, against him. Now come on, let's go."

I started jogging holding onto Leigh's hand. Once I felt sure she'd keep coming with me, I let go.

We kept moving deeper into the woods for about twenty minutes. The woods weren't thick and we'd traveled at a pretty good clip. I figured we'd gone about three klicks.

I was pleasantly surprised that Leigh had kept pace so well.

As we came to the edge of a small clearing, I held my arm straight back towards her with fingers up. That was the tactile hand signal for halt.

I guess some habits die hard.

"You doing all right?" I asked in a whisper.

She was breathing hard and despite the cool air, sweating.

"Yeah. You don't think he's left yet, do you?"

"Honestly? Yeah. I'm pretty sure he's left. I figure he went back into that building and grabbed one of those PowerBook portable computers. And then started after us."

"A computer? But why?"

"He's got cameras around these woods. Not a lot of them, but we've gone past three."

"But that's cheating!"

I laughed. I couldn't help it.

"How many rich men ever played square?"

"So what do we do?"

"We keep moving."

We crossed the clearing. Then the woods thinned out. Actually, the area would have been perfect for a picnic.

But we kept on.

We'd passed only one more camera.

I hoped it would be the last. But I didn't have high hopes.

Off in the distance, I could see the walls of a canyon.

Normally, I would have veered away from a place where we could get trapped. But I could see a waterfall glistening in the noonday sun.

"There should be a river up ahead," I said. "We might be able to lose Willow by getting into the water and coming ashore someplace he can't see."

I was just starting to feel a little better about our chances when we suddenly rounded the bend.

Standing on his hind legs, as if he was waiting for us, was a bear.

And he was only about ten yards away.

Some type of deep-throated pulsing sound rumbled in his throat. I didn't know what it meant. But from the look on his face, he didn't look happy!

THIRTY-TWO

Joe tossed and turned that night, worried about Steel and Leigh Ellerton.

But he's a big boy, Joe thought hopefully.

After a restless night's sleep, morning finally came. Before Joe headed to work, he grabbed a quick bite of breakfast with his wife, Carolyn. Over coffee and a donut—yes, policemen really do like donuts—he told his wife about his conversation with Drew Harrison.

When he told her about his idea of how to catch the senator in the act, she told him she didn't think it would work.

The voice of reason?

"His parents will never let you use their child as a decoy."

"You may be right," Joe replied softly.

When Joe got to his desk that morning, he was pleased.

I guess my threat worked!

A folder containing the call logs from both Ellerton's and Steel's phones were inside. They'd originally been Xerox copies that had been faxed over. They weren't the best quality, but he was still able to read them.

As he looked at the phone numbers, nothing immediately stood out. Joe looked at the dates and was disappointed the records only went through the previous week. No record of who'd called who yesterday.

Dang it!

Joe called Officer Peter Sinclair.

"Pete, who's handling the Ellerton case?"

"Officer Estes."

"Good. Jim's a good man. Tell him I want to know anything he finds out immediately."

"Will do."

They hung up.

Switching gears, Joe reached for his Rolodex. He flipped it until he came to the "S" section and quickly found the number for Special Agent Robert Shaw of the F.B.I.

Wilson and Shaw had crossed paths a few times over the years. Joe liked working with the special agent because he'd never gotten into a pissing contest about who had jurisdiction over a case. Together, they realized that they both had a job to do and that there'd be plenty of credit to go around once they succeeded.

As the phone rang, Joe leaned back, crossed his feet, and stuck them on his desk.

"Special Agent Shaw,"

"Bob. It's Joe Wilson."

"Joe! How's it going?"

"You know, same old garbage, different day."

"I hear ya, brother."

"But, Bob, I do have a humdinger for you!"

That's when Joe told Shaw all about the Whitfield case.

"There's some type of dinner this Friday and the senator wants Drew there," Joe explained. "The kid has agreed to wear a wire."

"And you need me to provide it?"

"Well, D.C. is out of my jurisdiction," Joe replied. Then, "And after all, what're friends for?"

Shaw laughed. "I think I can provide you with the equipment."

"Thanks, Bob."

"The kid will have to be a wing walker," Shaw stated. "Cold and bold. Not to mention controlled."

"Well, after some convincing on my part, he's willing to give it a try," Joe replied. "But because he's a minor, we'll have to get his parents' permission."

"That's a good point. I imagine the odds aren't good. Parents aren't in the habit of putting their children in danger."

"Great! Now you sound like my wife."

"Huh?"

"Never mind," Joe said. He closed his eyes. "You wanna help me try to get their permission?" Joe asked hopefully. "I figure the face of the F.B.I., even your face, might convince them that their kid will be safe."

There was quite on the other end for a moment and Joe started to get a sinking feeling.

"Sure," Shaw said. "Why not? In for a penny, in for a pound."

"Thanks, Bob. I really appreciate it."

They agreed to meet at the Harrison house at seven o'clock that night.

THIRTY-THREE

"Freeze!" I hissed through gritted teeth. I put my hands out as if I were a safety patrol. "Don't run or he'll think we're prey."

"Well, dammit, we are!" Leigh squawked back.

The bear dropped down onto all fours and let out a growl that made the surrounding trees in the woods tremble.

Or maybe it was just my knees.

"Shit!" Leigh exclaimed.

"Stay calm," I said in a voice that was anything but.

"Easy for you to say."

Leigh started to turn.

"He can outrun you," I said.

"What're we supposed to do? Just stand here?"

"Actually, we're supposed to drop to the ground, take a fetal position, and cover our necks with our hands."

"Sounds like that we're supposed to bend over and kiss our asses goodbye!"

A quick smile flashed across my face. I couldn't help it. I recalled being in school in the 1950s when we were told to hide underneath our desks in case of a nuclear bomb exploding.

"I've got an idea," Leigh said.

Before I could ask what, she threw the hamburger and the bag of potato chips at the bear.

Then she turned and started to run.

I took a few steps backwards. I figured she had a better chance of making it if I just stayed and let the bear get me first.

But our furry friend went for the fast-food staple and, a few seconds later, I found myself running right behind Leigh.

"Well, there goes our food," I said breathlessly when we finally stopped.

"Better losing food than being food!" she retorted breathing hard.

"No, it was good thinking, Leigh. I remember reading somewhere that black bears have a sense of smell that's about seven times better than a dog's. He'd probably already smelled the hamburger!"

Leigh smiled.

Despite her hair being a mess, her makeup gone or smeared, and rivulets of sweat running down her face, she looked beautiful!

Damn! I got it bad.

"Now, let's get out of here!" I said, getting back to business.

Leigh and I took a wide berth around the bear and continued on towards the waterfall.

The sun was now directly over us. Even though we were protected by the shade of the trees, the morning coolness had burned off and had been replaced by the heat of the afternoon.

By now I'd lost track of how far we'd gone, maybe another two to three klicks.

We were starting to slow down from our brisk pace. Leigh had taken her jacket off and tied it around her waist.

"This is insanity!" she blurted.

"I agree. I think we need to find a safe place to hide you so I can circle back and take care of him."

Leigh stopped dead in her tracks. "You're not leaving me alone out here."

"Look. He brought you out here to slow me down."

As soon as the words came out of my mouth I knew I shouldn't have said them. I wanted to reach out and take them back.

"Oh, so I'm just some helpless woman tying you down?"

"No. Leigh, no, that's not what I meant."

"Well, it sure sounded like it. Maybe I should go my way and you go yours."

That actually isn't a bad idea. But if he went after you and you died, I'd never forgive myself.

Leigh started to walk away.

I didn't have time for this.

"Look, Leigh, he knows I care about you. He's counting on that to keep us together. And whether you like it or not, I'm a soldier and trained for this. You aren't a liability. You're the reason I want to survive. If you weren't here, I'd probably go straight for the guy and not care whether I live or die!"

Leigh started to tear up. She put a hand over her mouth.

Then the tears started streaking down her cheeks.

I walked up to her and put my arms around her.

She hugged me back, putting her head on my chest.

Leigh held me tightly.

"I'm so scared," she sobbed. "I have three kids and a husband and I'm not ready to die."

"You're not going to," I said firmly. "We're going to get you somewhere safe and then I'm going back for the bastard."

"And if he kills you?"

"That's not an option."

Suddenly, off in the distance, we heard the sound of a rifle going off, twice.

At the sound, Leigh cowered.

Thank heavens he doesn't have an automatic.

I didn't say it out loud. That was good. Sometimes I speak before I think and I didn't need to be putting bad ideas in Leigh's head!

"Come on," I said. "We've got to keep moving."

We took off again. This time our pace was once again at a fast clip.

"You think he killed the bear?" Leigh asked.

"That would be my guess."

"So somehow, in the middle of nowhere, he's still right behind us?"

"There are still cameras out here. Only I haven't seen one for the last klick or so."

"Klick?"

"It means kilometers."

"And how far is a klick?"

"Point six two of a mile."

"A little over half a mile?"

"Yes."

"Then why don't they just say that?"

I looked over at her. Leigh was smiling.

She's putting me on. That's a good sign!

I had to laugh "Because, it's the military, ma'am."

"Of course it is!" she laughed back.

Atta girl, Leigh, be brave!

As the afternoon passed, we kept moving along at a brisk clip. But it wasn't always easy over the rugged terrain.

I was impressed with Leigh. We only stopped once for a break.

"Here's some water," I said, handing her a canteen.

I would have told her not to drink too much. But if she ran out I would've given her my water.

As I watched her drink, I felt a wave of guilt overcome me.

"I'm sorry," I said.

"For what?"

"For getting you into this mess."

"It's not your fault. You didn't drag me here."

"But still."

"Hey!" she snapped. "It's not your fault we're friends." She paused. "Although I will admit, I'd rather be home."

I smiled. "I'd bet you'd rather be almost anywhere else."

She looked at me and I could see her mind churning. But I couldn't tell what she was thinking.

"Not necessarily," she said softly. "If I can help you out of this mess . . ."

I looked at her and could tell she meant it.

"You're a good friend," I said. And I meant it.

Willow had brought her here to slow me down. He didn't realize he'd given me a reason to live.

"How are you holding up in those shoes?" I asked.

Her dress shoes weren't exactly suited for hiking.

"Just a few blisters. But I'll live."

Leigh was one tough cookie!

We finished drinking our water, neither of us having more than a few gulps.

"Let's saddle up," I said and we continued on.

Finally, we could hear the roar of a waterfall from somewhere up ahead.

Soon afterwards we came to a clearing. Off in the distance was the canyon wall with a waterfall cutting through its side.

And at the base was a river.

We'd gotten to our goal!

"Now what?" Leigh asked.

"Now we're going to lose Willow!"

THIRTY-FOUR

Joe pulled up in front of the Harrison house about ten minutes early. He wasn't surprised to find that Bob Shaw was already there. Joe knew that Shaw was a believer in the adage, "If you're not early, you're late."

Joe looked at his watch.

We might as well head in. After all, we aren't expected at any certain time.

Joe climbed out of his car while Shaw got out of a black, federally-issued SUV.

The special agent started walking over towards Joe.

Bob Shaw was in his late 40s. He had whitish-blond hair. The smattering of gray in it reflected light and acted as highlights. Bob was average height with a wiry build. He was wearing a blue suit, white shirt, and red tie. Even though the sun was starting to set, he wore sunglasses. You know, the standard Fed look.

"Special Agent Shaw," Joe said, tipping his fedora as he walked toward the man.

"Detective Wilson," Bob returned formally.

At the sound of their titles Joe laughed, "Boy, aren't we special?"

"No, I'm special. You're just a detective," Shaw chuckled.

Smiling, they firmly grasped hands and shook.

"Good to see you."

"You too. It's been a while."

"Thanks for coming."

"Do you know what you're going to say?" Shaw asked.

"I have some talking points. But no, I'm just winging it. You?"

"No. Like you. I'm flying by the seat of my pants."

Together, they headed up the walk to the Harrisons' house.

As they neared the front door Joe said, "My kids used to love pushing elevator buttons and doorbells." He smiled and stuck his hand out as if presenting something. "Be my guest."

Shaw laughed and pushed the doorbell.

"Calling me immature or young at heart?" Shaw asked, returning the banter.

"The former?"

"Yeah, well for your information, I don't let my kids push the buttons. I do it!"

"Father of the year," Joe joked.

"Naw. Just *special* father of the year," Bob corrected with a smile and a wink.

Both men pulled their creds.

A middle-aged man came to the front door. He was dressed in slacks, a light blue shirt with a dark blue plaid tie pulled loosely away from his unbuttoned collar.

He'd obviously just gotten home from work.

He was tall and skinny with a pronounced Adam's apple. His hair was dyed a blackish-brown, He sort of looked like a burnt matchstick. He wore slightly tinted aviator glasses. And behind those lenses, his eyes grew concerned at the sight of the two men standing on his front porch. In their suits, Fedora and sunglasses, they looked like cops straight out of Central Casting.

"Can I help you?"

"Mr. Harrison?" Shaw asked.

"Yes," he answered cautiously.

"I'm Bob Shaw of the F.B.I. This is Detective Joe Wilson of the Fairfax County Police Department."

"Is something wrong?"

"We'd like to come in and talk to you about your son, Drew."

The man's face fell.

"He hasn't don't anything wrong, sir," Joe added quickly.

The man looked dazed, as if someone had hit him over the head with a baseball bat. "Umm, okay."

As he held the door open for the two men he said, "I'm Henry Harrison, Drew's dad."

Once inside the house, a woman walked out of the kitchen, drying her hands on a dishtowel.

"Henry?" she asked uncertainly.

Uh, this is my wife, Esther.

She's not an Esther. Joe thought. *She's a Sophia!* He meant as in Sophia Loren. *She's absolutely gorgeous!*

And she was.

Esther was short with dark delicate features. Her black shoulder length hair was parted down the middle. Her long bangs were feathered past her ocean blue eyes. She had high cheekbones, full lips and straight white teeth.

She was middle-aged. But she was one of the most beautiful women Joe had even seen.

A rare jewel.

Can you tell Joe was smitten?

"This is Mr. Shaw and Detective Wilson," Henry introduced. "They're here to talk about Drew."

"What!" Esther gasped, alarmed.

"He hasn't don't anything wrong, ma'am," Joe added quickly, once again.

"Oh?" she asked, still anxious.

"If we could sit down and talk," Joe said. "We can explain."

They all headed into the living room.

Joe made a bee-line for the recliner. Shaw sat down in an overstuffed chair as the concerned couple sat down on a matching sofa.

"It would probably be best if you called your son," Shaw stated. "Please."

Henry stood up again and walked to the base of the stairs.

"Drew? Could you please come down here?"

Henry sat back down next to his wife. A moment later, Drew came downstairs and entered the living room. He stood there for a moment and stared at the guests.

"Hey, Drew," Joe said, standing, shaking hands. "It's good to see you again. This is Special Agent Bob Shaw of the F.B.I."

Shaw stood and shook the boy's hand.

"Please, take a seat," Joe said.

Drew sat down next to his parents on the sofa.

Because Joe had already talked with the boy, he took the lead.

"Mr. and Mrs. Harrison, there are some rumors about Senator Frank Lindsey that we are investigating. I've talked to Drew and he's agreed to help us with the investigation."

"What? What do you mean? What's going on?" Henry asked.

"There are rumors that the senator is being inappropriate with his male interns."

Both of the older Harrisons turned and looked at their son.

"Has something happened?" Esther asked.

From the tone of her voice, she sounded horrified.

"No. Well, at least not yet," Drew answered. "He's rubbed my shoulder and back a few times. He seems awfully chummy to me compared to others. And he really wants me to be at this employee dinner this Friday. And . . ."

"And Drew has agreed to wear a wire," Joe finished.

"What? No!" Henry Harrison exclaimed. "I will not allow my son to be put into danger!"

Esther nodded her head in agreement.

"He won't be in danger," Shaw stated firmly. He motioned to Joe. "We're both fathers. We'd never let anything happen to a child. Right Joe?"

Inwardly, Joe cringed at the statement. He'd buried his son, Joey, just the previous month. Joey had been murdered in retaliation for an arrest Joe had made years earlier. And then the convict had escaped prison. Steel had captured the killer . . .

I couldn't protect my own boy!

"Joe?"

"Huh?"

"We'd never let anything happen to their son."

"Oh. No. Of course not!"

"Now, wait," Henry said, throwing his hands up. "Where'd the rumors come from?"

"A previous intern," Joe replied.

"So why isn't he testifying?"

Joe and Bob looked at each other.

Bob gave a slight nod. Neither one of them had wanted it to get to this point.

Joe spoke softly. "Umm, well, because he's dead. He was murdered."

You know the old saying, 'You could've heard a pin drop'? Well, it's appropriate here. Because time seemed to freeze for a millisecond as the Harrisons tried to process what Joe had said.

"He was murdered?" Drew's father finally echoed.

"Yes. And we need to stop the people responsible."

"And the senator did it?"

"No, his people did. Now whether he knew about it or not is still open to debate."

"I want to help, Dad," Drew said. "If I can catch the senator trying to do something inappropriate, we can arrest him and maybe have him flip on who did kill the intern."

"His name was Cody Whitfield," Joe said. "Like your boy, he was just sixteen."

Esther shook her head. "We'd like to help, but we just can't. Drew's our son and as you said, you're parents. You would never willingly put your child in danger."

"But Mom," Drew protested. "You and Dad always taught me the best thing you can do in life is make a difference, to help people. That's why I want to become a politician."

He looked at his parents. "If I wear a wire, I'd be making a difference and making sure that those responsible will never do it again."

Esther put her head in her hands and started to cry.

She knew what was coming.

She'd been an anti-war protester at Kent State in 1970. She was a freshman when the Ohio National Guard came in and shot into a crowd of students, killing four and wounding nine.

Almost two years earlier, Henry had been in Chicago during the 1968 Democratic National Convention as an anti-war protester. He'd been part of the march that had demonstrated throughout the city. That is, until Chicago's Mayor Daley brought in 23,000 police and National Guardsman to violently crush the 10,000 protesters.

Henry had gotten battered, bruised, and arrested for his troubles.

Drew's parents had tried to make a difference.

And Ester and Henry weren't hypocrites. They believed in doing right.

"You better damn well take care of our son!" Henry growled.

THIRTY-FIVE

Leigh and I walked briskly toward the waterfall.

To my surprise, as we got closer to the river, I spotted a cabin off to the side.

"Look at that!" Leigh exclaimed a split second later. "A cabin!"

She started for it.

"Hold up," I said, grabbing her arm and leading her back toward the safety of the woods. "We've got to be careful."

"You think someone's in there?"

The cabin itself looked dilapidated and deserted. But you never know.

"I'm sure Willow knows about the cabin," I said. "He'd never let us simply walk to safety or let us benefit from anything out here."

"You're probably right," Leigh agreed.

"I think we should stay away from it. I don't want to risk running into a friend of his who might hold us captive or send us back into the bastard's hands at gunpoint."

Leigh and I walked along the edge of the woods toward the river, looking toward the cabin for any signs of life.

We didn't see any.

Leigh and I came out at the river's edge about a hundred yards down from the waterfall.

We stood there looking at the water.

"Okay," I said. "You're not going to like this, but we've got to get into the river so that we can lose Willow. For all I know he's got a bloodhound."

I was expecting her to protest. But instead, she said, "Peachy."

"What?"

"Peachy."

I had to laugh. Leigh knew I liked to kid around and say that I was on a one-man crusade to bring back that word. And I appreciated her sense of humor by saying it now.

"Okay," I said. "It's going to be cold as fu . . . umm, heck."

"If fuck is cold," she said. "Then maybe you're doing it wrong!"

This time we both laughed.

"Do we take our shoes off?" she asked, looking down into the fast moving water.

"I'm not," I replied. "I don't know how deep the water is, but I'm just planning to walk along the shore. I'm hoping we won't have to swim."

"Okay," she said uncertainly. Then, "Just a sec."

Leigh untied her jacket from her waist and put it on. Then she buttoned it.

When she was ready, I stepped off the bank and down into the river. The water was about six inches below the bank.

As I stepped in, I really wished I'd chosen my combat boots instead of my Nikes.

The water was cold. A lot colder than the rivers I'd waded through in Vietnam. Sometimes they were as warm as piss.

"Yep, it's cold," I warned.

I held my hand out and Leigh grabbed it.

"Whew!" she exclaimed as she stepped into the river. "It is cold as fuck!"

"Well, then you're doing it wrong," I quipped.

A woman that can drop the f-bomb so sweetly—what's not to love?

I was going to let go of her hand but she held on tightly.

Suddenly my feet weren't so cold.

We were about calf deep in the river as we started walking with the current.

We slogged along the shore line, trying not to kick water up on each other.

"Keep an eye out for Willow," I said. "We might have to slip down into the water if we see him."

"Chilling," Leigh deadpanned.

I liked the way she was handling the situation. Showing fear wouldn't help anybody.

While we kept an eye out for Willow, I also paid attention to the trees along the closer bank.

It didn't take me long to find what I was looking for.

I let go of Leigh's hand and turned to face her. I'd been dreading this moment.

"Okay," I said. "This is my plan."

She looked up at me expectantly.

"You're going up that tree right there," I said, pointing.

It was tall. The lower twenty feet or so had no limbs. Then, the top part branched out into a thick canopy of foliage. It was just like all the other trees around. But the reason I'd picked it was because the tree was right beside the river.

It'd be easy to hide our tracks.

"When you're up there, Willow won't be able to see you," I said. "You'll be safe!"

"Are you crazy?" Leigh exclaimed. "I can't climb a tree!"

"I'm doing the climbing. Your job is to hold onto me."

Leigh looked at me as if I'd lost my mind. Then she said, "You really mean it, don't you?"

I nodded my head.

"When you're safe, I'm going after Willow."

"And if you don't get him?"

"That's not an option," I stated firmly.

We waded to shore. The roots of the tree overhung the river-bank like a spider's web.

I stepped on them and climbed out of the water. Then I reached down and pulled Leigh up.

"Okay," I said as I walked to the base of the tree. "I'm going to kneel down. You put one arm over my shoulder, the other under my arm. Then reach around and grasp your wrists, hands, whatever works for you. You can wrap your legs around me, but it's probably best you do that after I've shimmied up the lower part."

She nodded her head dumbly at me.

"If at any time you think you're losing your grip, tell me and I'll slide down."

"Okay."

"Once we make the branches, it should be smooth sailing."

"Except for one thing."

"What?"

"I'm afraid of heights."

I tried to hide it, but I'm sure my face gave away my disap-pointment.

"But," she said a moment later. "This is as good as any time to face my fears, right?"

"If you can't do it, then we won't."

"Look, I don't like to think of myself as a liability. I'd much rather be by your side and help you fight this psycho. But if you think this is our option for surviving, then I'll do what you say. After all, you're the soldier."

For some reason, at that moment I was overcome with emotion. I reached out and gave her a hug.

She hugged back and held on tightly.

As we drew apart I looked down at her and said, "Ready?"

She nodded her head and took a big breath. "Let's do it!"

I knelt down and she put her arms around me.

I stood up and she rose off the ground.

"Hold on," I said. "Here we go."

I put my arms around the tree and wrapped my legs around the base. Then I started to shimmy up the tree.

The bark tore into my skin, but it wasn't too bad.

It seemed like Leigh had a strong grip. She hung off me like a cape.

I'd climbed trees wearing sixty-pound backpacks before. Leigh probably weighed double that. And I won't lie. It wasn't easy climbing the tree.

"Doing okay?" I asked.

"Yep," she grunted.

Her arm was crushing the side of my neck. It was hard to breath and it'd probably leave a mark.

A mark on my neck from Leigh Ellerton! I can't wait to show it off!

It's funny what the brain comes up with sometimes.

Truthfully though, I was worried about her slipping and falling. But her grip seemed strong as I climbed as quickly as I could.

A picture of Tarzan flashed through my mind.

I'll have to tell Joe about this . . . If we survive.

It didn't take long until I was pulling us up into the lower canopy of branches.

Once there, I turned in a way so that Leigh could easily slip off my back and sit safely on a branch.

"That wasn't so bad," I said as I turned to her.

Leigh was as white as a ghost.

"You okay?" I asked, reaching out and touching her shoulder.

"Y-yes," she stammered nervously.

She looked at me. "Are you okay?"

"Sure, why?"

"Your neck has a mark on it. It's bruised, like a hippo gave you a hickey or something."

I reached up and touched it and laughed. "The other animals will be so jealous."

Leigh smiled and I took that as a good sign.

"Let's climb up," I said. "Once you're surrounded by branches and leaves, you won't be able to see the ground and maybe that'll make you feel better."

"Okay," she said meekly.

"You go first," I said. "I'll be right behind you, protecting you. You'll be safe."

And she would be. I wasn't about to let anything happen to her. I was damn well determined to make sure her kids got their mother back!

The going was very slow as Leigh tentatively climbed the tree.

The limbs were thick at this level and the climbing was easy.

As we went higher, the branches thinned out.

By now we were so high up that the tree was starting to sway back and forth in the breeze.

"How's this?" she asked hopefully.

"If you could go just a little bit further up. See where the tree splits into a U?"

She looked up.

"I think you could straddle that and be safe," I said.

"How long are you planning to desert me?"

That hurt. I wasn't deserting her. At least as far as I was concerned.

"I'll be back as soon as I can," I said. "I promise."

She started back up the tree. "If I spend the night up here, I might fall once I'm asleep."

I'd already thought of that and, again, she wasn't going to like my idea.

We continued on in silence.

Leigh climbed up to the U in the tree and straddled it.

Up here, the tree swayed gently and the green sun-drenched leaves rattled like castanets. It would've been quite beautiful and peaceful if we weren't so high up in the air.

I looked down. You couldn't see a thing. The ground and surroundings were covered like a blanket by the tree's thick foliage.

Willow will never see her.

I felt happy that he wouldn't be able to pick her off like a sniper.

"I was thinking you should probably take your belt off," I suggested. "I'll tie your hands together, snugly, but not so tight that you can't wiggle free. That way if you sleep, you won't fall."

Leigh looked at me as if I was a few bulbs short of a chandelier.

But a moment later she said, "Okay. That makes sense."

She kept a death grip on a branch as she used her other hand to unbuckle her belt. Then she pulled it free from the belt loops.

"Here," she said and handed it to me.

I took the braided belt and handed her a canteen. I then maneuvered so that I was on the opposite side. She hugged the tree and put her wrists side by side.

I tied her hands together.

"Can you work your way out of this?" I asked.

She wiggled her arms. "Yes."

"Do you want me to give you a drink before I leave?"

"No, I'll pull a hand out when I want a drink."

"Do you feel safe?"

Reluctantly she nodded her head.

I saw tears start to well up in her eyes. When they rolled down her face, I took my hand and gently wiped her cheeks.

"I'm proud of you," I said. "Thank you."

I bent over and kissed her on her wet cheek.

Suddenly, I felt like maybe I had done something wrong.

But she didn't act like I had.

"Come back for me soon," she said desperately.

"As soon as I can. I promise."

We took one last look at each other.

We both knew it might be the last time we'd ever see each other.

I felt sick.

With a nod, I started down from the tree.

THIRTY-SIX

Despite the fact it was almost 8 P.M. when Joe left the Harrisons' house, he headed back to his office.

As usual it was all quiet during the night shift. The detective's area was deserted. Joe liked it that way. He wouldn't have to be "social."

He sat down at his desk and saw a small pile of pink papers.

They were phone messages.

He hoped they contained information from Officer Estes on Gary's disappearance.

I could use some good news about now.

But when he picked up the messages and shuffled through them, his heart sank. There were three messages and all of them were from George Ellerton.

Dammit. And I've got nothing for him.

Suddenly, Officer Estes came walking in.

He looked weary. Even his red hair seemed to have lost some of its luster.

"You're here," Estes said, surprised.

"Yes. But what're you still doing here?" Joe asked.

Estes was off the clock at five.

"Tying up loose ends and I wanted to write you a note about the Ellerton case."

Joe nodded his head expectantly.

"I canvassed the neighborhood this afternoon. All I got was a neighbor seeing a white van pulling out of the Ellerton's garage at 8:35. They had the exact time because they were heading out to work."

"Any markings on the van?"

"No, sir."

Unknowingly, Joe gritted his teeth and made a fist.

"I spent this evening looking at video from traffic cameras. I found a plain white van heading west on Ox Road a few minutes after the neighbor had spotted it. I couldn't be sure that it was the same one of course. But I went ahead and ran the license plate. It turns out the vehicle is from a car rental place in Fairfax. I called them and got a name, Percy Willow. According to DMV he's a male, Caucasian, age forty-four. I did a quick background check on him. He seems clean."

"Any idea where the van is?"

"No, sir."

"By chance does it have Lojack?"

Estes shook his head. "I asked. No, the system is too cost prohibited to put in rentals."

Joe nodded his head. "You got an address for this Willow?"

Estes pulled a piece of paper out of the file he was holding.

"Here's a copy of his driver's license."

"Excellent work, Officer Estes!" said as he took it. "Thank you!"

"Well, sir, we don't know if it's the right van. There're a lot of them out there on the road. Ironically, not as many without logos though. The van may have turned off the main road before I saw it on the traffic cam."

"Regardless. I want to talk to this Willow fellow. It's all we've got."

"Yes, sir. Do you want me to go with you?"

"No. You head home. You've done enough for one day. Thank you."

"Yes, sir."

Joe watched Estes leave. He had a sense of pride being part of the Fairfax County Police Department.

I work with good men.

Joe realized that Estes had stayed late, missed dinner with his family, and hadn't gotten paid for it.

He decided he'd have to see if he could get a few hours of overtime approved for the officer.

Joe picked up the phone and dialed the Ellertons' home number.

"Hello?"

The phone was hastily picked up on the first ring.

"Mr. Ellerton, this is Joe Wilson."

"Detective, is there any word on my wife?"

"No, sir. No word on her. But we are following a lead . . ."

Joe filled him in on what he knew.

"Have you thought of any reason why anyone would take your wife?" Joe asked when he'd concluded his recap.

There was silence on the other end of the line. "No, detective, none."

That's what I was afraid of. I'd bet this has something to do with Gary.

"I have to get back to work," Joe said. "Let me know if you hear anything."

THIRTY-SEVEN

Before I slid down the last part of the tree, I stood on the lowest limb and looked around.

The coast was clear. I didn't see or hear anything.

I went down the last part of the tree like a fireman sliding down a pole.

My instincts told me that Willow would be over in the direction we'd come.

Before I left, I looked up the tree. I couldn't see Leigh. But I felt a deep pang of duty toward the woman. I needed to save her at all costs. Up to now, in every life-threatening situation I'd ever encountered, the only life at stake was mine and mine alone.

And I didn't care.

But this time it was different. I had to save her life, even if it meant sacrificing my own.

I stepped into the river and glided down into the cold water. Then I started silently swimming upstream.

With the frigid water and night setting in, I was going to get cold.

But from my training I knew I'd be okay. As always it would be mind over matter.

As I swam I felt very guilty. How could I leave Leigh all alone up a tree? That was horrible.

Maybe I should go back and get her? We can stay together during the night and then separate again in the morning.

I thought about going back.

But then I realized Willow might have night vision glasses and if he did, he'd be able to pick us off one at a time.

I can't go back. I'd be putting her in danger.

I was just going to have to allow my friend to spend a night in hell . . .

I reached the other side of the river. A wall of rock towered above me. The sun reflected brightly off the whitish stone, making me feel like I was in a big spotlight.

It was sort of cool.

Suddenly part of the wall exploded above my head sending shards or rock raining down on me like a sudden hail storm.

I was being fired at!

Stupid!

How could I have acted so cavalierly? Like Willow wouldn't be somewhere watching!

I plunged down into the water, my muscles straining.

Bullets whizzed by, all around like angry hornets!

I could hear my heart pounding in my ears.

I swam to the bottom of the river and quickly debated whether I should turn around and swim along with the current to get as far away as possible.

But I knew I couldn't get far enough away. I'd still be an easy target. I decided to stay put. With Willow's eyes moving along with the current and me staying in the same place, maybe I could throw him off long enough to grab a big breath of air and swim as far as I could underwater.

I opened my eyes in the murky green water and I swam for the wall. Water rushed past my face.

If only I can find something to hold onto.

I reached out for the rock, but I felt nothing!

I looked and all I saw was inky blackness. Confused, I put my hand in it.

It felt cold.

A cave?

I was running out of air and I had to make a choice. Surface and risking getting my brains blown out, or go into the cave and possibly drown.

There was no time to debate. With a surge of power I kicked and used my arms to shoot forward into the darkness.

THIRTY-EIGHT

I shot into the dark cave, my arms stretched out in front of me. My fingers danced along the rock as I felt the sides angling inward.

After a bit, things got tighter still.

I started to get a bad feeling. I may have made the wrong decision.

This isn't a cave at all!

I was just about to turn around and pray that I had enough air to make it to the surface when I saw a glimmer of light straight ahead.

I zeroed in on it and angled up.

As I did, my head smashed into the rock ceiling.

I became woozy. With pain shooting through my head, the pounding of my heart in my ears, and my lungs aching and ready to burst, I frantically felt for the hole overhead. When I found it, I stuck my head through.

As my face hit air, I involuntarily exhaled and gasped at the same time, choking.

I'd made it! With my head spinning I gratefully took in a huge lungful of fresh air.

Without thinking, I wedged myself against a slimy, moss-covered ledge in the small chamber as I greedily gulped in breath after breath.

Water ran off my face as I realized that this had probably been the closest I'd ever gotten to dying. Well, I guess that is, if you don't count people shooting at me.

As I continued to breathe hard, I looked up. My head was in a small opening that angled on up into the rock. I couldn't see the sky, but the opening probably wasn't too far away.

It didn't matter though. The crevice wasn't big enough for me to climb through, unless I was the size of a five-year-old, I guess.

You're stuck between a rock and a head place.

The mind comes up with the strangest things sometimes. Here I was in a cramped chamber and my brain was butchering old sayings!

In the dim light I noticed that there were water rings that faded the further they went up. There was also a dark groove cut into the rock where it was apparent water ran down from the opening above.

I need to stay in here until it gets dark.

That would be a couple more hours.

If I'd been claustrophobic, I would've been in for a tough time. But I wasn't. I just closed my eyes and went to my happy place.

I pictured myself on a beach.

I could hear the roar of the waves and feel the warmth of the sun on my face. I wiggled my toes in the sand and pictured girls in bikinis walking along the shore. After a while, I imagined myself lying down on a blanket to take a nap. With warmth on my back, I started to tan.

Yes, the beach, my happy place.

I fully intended to wait in the dank crevice until dark. But the water was cold and not being able to move around and get the blood circulating didn't help. I started to shiver.

I've always preferred the heat to the cold.

After a while, my shivering got so bad that my whole body shook like a skeleton tap-dancing.

I've got to get out of here.

I opened my eyes. I don't know how long I'd been in la-la land. But I knew it hadn't been that long. It was still light outside, although I had the feeling that the shadows were starting to get long.

I can't wait until dark.

I knew I was going to have to risk going out there or freeze to death in here.

I hoped Willow thought he'd nabbed me and had moved on.

That certainly would help.

I started to hyperventilate, taking in deep breaths of air. I wanted to oxygenate my blood the best I could.

I took one last deep breath and dropped down into the water.

Normally I would've reared back, coiled my legs, and pushed off the rock with enough force to get me going at full-speed. But, since I couldn't see a thing and didn't want to slam into anything, I just dropped down into the water and started to swim with one arm out in front of me.

I don't know if you've ever swam in your clothes before, but they weigh you down like a lead jacket. It didn't matter though. I was a strong swimmer. You couldn't be a Navy SEAL if you weren't.

Once out into the river I turned right and continued low along the wall. I shot through the water swiftly using an underwater breaststroke. My body started to warm up as my muscles exploded stroke after stroke.

I was heading for the waterfall about one hundred yards away.

Fortunately I didn't have to surface. Air wasn't a problem.

I heard the rumbling sound in the water before I saw it. It got louder the closer I got.

As I swam, I had to be careful because the smooth mud floor had given a way to rocks and boulders.

For safety's sake, I rose up to just below the surface.

By now the noise was deafening. It sounded like the applause from a thunderous standing ovation.

Finally, up ahead, I could see the white foam from the crashing water of the falls.

I went underneath it and it was like getting a thousand slaps on the back at once.

It hurt.

I surfaced behind the waterfall and wiped my face.

There was room behind the falls to take a breath, but not much else.

I gulped in air and looked around. I was hoping there might be a place to hide back here, a place that I could bring Leigh to.

The light was dim behind the falls and I couldn't see real well. There didn't appear to be any place to hide.

Dammit!

I took a moment and then edged over to the side of the walls.

Well, this is it. If he knows you're here, you're dead.

I slowly stuck my head out.

Off in the distance the sun was just starting to set.

I looked across the river.

I didn't see anyone.

I climbed all the way out from behind the falls and turned around. I started to climb up the sheer cliff wall.

About halfway up, and about ten yards off to the side, I saw a small ledge.

I went for it.

It was tricky and I almost slipped and fell. But I finally made it and pulled myself up to safety.

It was a perfect little spot. It was about six feet long by four feet deep at its widest. I could spend the night here.

I crouched down behind a rock and looked out across the river.

I didn't see anything. No movement, nothing.

I stood up and started to take my clothes off.

The chill of night was starting to set in and I needed to get out of my wet clothes.

Standing there naked, I took each item of clothing and held it over the rock and wrung it out like a washcloth.

I'd done my tee-shirt, socks and underwear before I started on my jeans.

As I twisted one of my pants legs, I felt something small.

Hmm, a pebble must've got in there.

I flipped the leg back and forth like a whip over the rock ledge.

To my surprise, when I felt the spot again, the lump was still there.

I turned the pants leg inside out and looked. To my shock there was a small patch ironed onto the fabric.

Alarmed, I tore at the sides with my fingers.

I managed to loosen a corner and pulled at it with a finger-nail.

The fabric pulled away and a small metal object fell into my hand.

A tracker!

I'd wondered how Willow could've possibly tracked us in this vast wilderness. My first theory had been the security cameras we'd seen earlier. But after a few klicks I hadn't seen any. Then I figured that he must have had a bloodhound. That made as much sense to me as anything.

Now I knew. He'd tagged us while we were unconscious.

Leigh!

My eyes must've bugged out when I finally figured out what two plus two equaled.

I pulled on my damp clothes as quickly as I could, all the while checking for more trackers.

There were none.

Let me tell you, it's not easy putting on wet clothes. Especially when you're in a hurry!

Sitting down, the shoes were the last thing I put on. Before I did, I turned them upside down and poured the water out of them.

If the situation wasn't so dire, I might've laughed.

As I got to my feet, I thought of stepping on the tracker. However, that'd be stupid. You don't let your enemy know you're onto him, especially when he's a psychotic sicko like this guy.

I also considered throwing the tracker into the river and let it float downstream. However, that was the direction I was heading in. Since I didn't want to tip Willow off, I decided it was just best to leave the tracker on the rocky ledge.

I looked out over the river. Remembering where the rocks were, I stepped back. My muscles tensed and then exploded. I ran and dove out over the water.

I could hear the wind whistle past my ears on the long drop. I hit the water hard and it stung the top of my head. Once in the water, I angled my body in such a way that I wouldn't go too far down.

I shot to the top of the river.

Once again I was icy cold. But this time I didn't really notice. It was because I didn't have time to care.

I started swimming toward the other side of the river.

A moment later I was on my feet, sloshing my way up the bank.

I took a quick look over my shoulder. I checked the deserted house. No one was in sight.

Across the river the waterfall grabbed my attention. An orange blaze of color reflected off the water making it look like it was on fire.

Yep. I'm in hell.

It reminded me of pictures I'd seen of Yosemite's El Capitan Waterfall. The setting sun hitting it in such a way that it looked like it was actually burning.

Now, the sun was playing the same trick here, only on a smaller scale. Honestly, the view was breathtaking. Only I didn't have time to enjoy the sights.

I put my head down and started running toward Leigh.

THIRTY-NINE

Before he left the station, Joe looked at a map and wrote down directions to Willow's house.

It was getting late—well, late to be dropping in unannounced.

But sometimes that worked best on an unsuspecting subject.

As he drove down the street where Willow lived, he immediately realized that the man was well off. Very well off!

He should've known that when he'd looked up the address.

You're slipping, Wilson.

Suddenly, Willow didn't seem like the type of guy who'd kidnap someone.

Having money will do that for a guy.

But Joe decided he'd come this far, he might as well see it through.

He pulled up to a gate. Off in the distance he could see a mansion. He didn't see any cars around, much less a white van.

There was fancy garden lighting around the property and Joe could tell the grounds were well manicured.

At least that's how it appeared in the dim light.

The house itself was mostly dark, with the exception of just a few lights.

Joe pressed a button on a metal pad.

A moment later a male voice crackled from a small mounted speaker. "May I help you?"

"Yes, I'm Detective Joe Wilson," he said as he held his creds out toward the camera. "I'd like to talk to a Percy Willow."

Joe had purposely left out that he was with the Fairfax County Police Department.

He had no jurisdiction here in McLean.

"I'm afraid Mr. Willow is not home."

"Well, then, can I speak to his wife?"

"There is no Mrs. Willow."

Joe sat in his idling car for a moment. "May I ask who you are?"

"My name is Stamford. I am Mr. Willow's butler."

"Butler? I didn't know they still had those."

Joe's crack was met with silence.

"When will Mr. Willow be back?"

"He is away on a business trip. I do not know exactly when he'll return."

"Thanks," Joe said.

He'd physically and metaphorically hit a dead-end.

He put the car in reverse, turned around, and headed for home.

That night, as an exhausted Joe Wilson put his head down on his pillow, he had one thought: *Gary, where are you?*

FORTY

I ran the first quarter mile at full speed.

Then I slowed down. I felt I had to be cautious now. It wouldn't do me any good to run into a hail of bullets.

The sun was below the horizon but it was still light out.

I crept quietly along the riverbank, my senses alert.

Then I came to a little inlet.

Looking around, I stepped down into it and grabbed a handful of dark brown mud. I started to rub it on my face. I didn't have a camo stick. But this would do.

I was working the mud over my exposed arms when I smelled it.

Cigarette smoke!

I immediately dropped and rolled.

But it was too late. A gun went off and I felt the force of a bullet tear into my upper left arm.

At first I didn't feel anything. A moment later I felt a searing burning. Then, finally, I felt pain.

While all of this was happening, I looked up.

Willow stood there with a smile on his face. "I'd hoped for more from you," he said, matter-of-factly. "But it is what it is."

"Well, maybe if you hadn't put trackers on us," I yelled loudly, sounding like some type of lunatic. "A real man wouldn't cheat!"

I hoped that somehow Leigh could hear me and find her tracker. Maybe she'd have a chance if he couldn't trace her.

Then a sick thought ran through my mind and chilled me to the bone.

What if he's already killed her!

But I hadn't heard gunshots.

"Whatever," Willow replied to my insult.

He casually raised the rifle's sight to his eye.

So this is how it ends.

I was deciding which way I should dive when suddenly I saw a blur as a wild shriek split the air.

Willow lost his balance and went down hard. He dropped his rifle as he fell into the inlet with me.

Leigh Ellerton on top!

What the . . . ?

I didn't have time to think. I just reacted, jumping into action.

Anger swept through me like a tornado. I lost it and went berserk. My fist started pounding Willow's face. The sound of broken bones seemed to excite me with bloodlust.

I continued pounding him mercilessly.

I can't let him hurt Leigh!

I was like an automated sledge hammer, punching him again and again.

"He's dead!" Leigh screamed as she threw herself on my back and tried to pull me off. "Gary, he's dead."

I hadn't realized that the side of his skull was against a rock.

The back part of his head had caved in and his face was distorted and a mess of bloody goo.

On wobbly knees I stood up and looked down at him.

Willow had a backpack and canteen strapped to his back.

Cheater!

I swayed from side-to-side and Leigh put an arm around me.

I looked at her and asked, "Are you all right?"

She nodded her head.

From the look on her face I figured she was disgusted with me. But instead, she said. "You've been shot."

Oh yeah.

I looked down at my arm. Blood had spider-webbed its way down my triceps and bicep. It was now dripping on the ground.

"How'd you get here?" I asked, ignoring my wound.

"Come on," she said as she took me by my good arm. "Let's get out of here. I can't take looking at that piece of shit's face any longer. I need to fix you up."

Together we climbed out of the little inlet and started walking along the banks of the river. We headed toward the deserted cabin.

When we'd gone a little bit, Leigh stopped and said, "Let me look at that."

She lifted the blood drenched sleeve of my tee-shirt.

She leaned in and looked closely at the wound.

"It appears to have gone through."

"Good," I replied. "It's just a flesh wound. Let's keep going."

"No, I've got to clean you up," she insisted. "I don't want you to get an infection."

As she took her jacket off I said, "You saved me."

She looked at me. "No problem."

A liability indeed!

"Maybe you should wash that mud off first."

For what seemed like the umpteenth time I went into the cold river.

I stood there and bent over. I washed my face, hands, and arms, being careful around the gunshot wound.

"How'd you'd come to be here?" I asked as I climbed back out.

"I took a drink and accidentally dropped my canteen. So I climbed down to get it. I saw Willow off in the distance walking towards me. I hid in some bushes. I noticed he was looking at something. It looked like some type of portable TV. That's when I realized he must've put a tracker on me."

I nodded my head.

Atta girl!

"I frantically checked my clothes and found it. I pulled it out and threw it away. Then I started following him. I hoped he would lead me to you."

"You were right," I said proudly.

Leigh had torn the thin lining out of her jacket. She wetted it with water from her canteen and started cleaning the wound.

As she blotted around it she said, "This is going to hurt. The bullet took a big chunk out of you."

"Naw, it's mind over matter—"

"If you don't mind, it doesn't matter," she finished with a laugh.

She cleaned out the wound and I gritted my teeth. Ultimately, she made a bandage with the rest of her coat's lining and tied it over the wound.

"There. Hopefully that will keep infection from setting in."

"Thank you," I said.

Then, together, we walked off into the growing darkness of night.

FORTY-ONE

We made it back to the cabin. It was deserted with nothing inside but dirt and grime. It appeared that no one had lived there for a long time. In fact, part of the roof had rotted away.

Leigh and I slept next to each other, trying to stay warm. Being out of the wind helped.

To my surprise we slept pretty well. I guess we were both exhausted.

Our stomachs growled and both of us were starved when we woke up. But since we didn't have any food, we didn't talk about it.

Leigh and I had nursed the water in our canteens and each of us had some left.

Still, it wasn't much. I offered to go get Willow's canteen, but Leigh didn't want me going anywhere near the dead man.

"We'll be fine," she said, shaking her canteen.

We gathered our things and started the hike back to Willow's compound.

I guess if this was a horror movie, Willow would've been standing outside the door, waiting for us. His distorted face, still oozing goo, would break out into a skeletal smile as he gunned us down.

Fortunately, he was nowhere to be seen.

Of course he wasn't!

The sun was just rising over the mountains when we started out. The coldness of the night slowly dissolved in the warmth of daylight.

"

As we ventured onward, I felt closer to Leigh than I had to any other woman, ever.

I knew I was in love. I had been for a long time.

We talked as we walked along. After a while I finally got the courage to say, "I really like you, Leigh."

"I really like you too, Gary."

For a moment I thought I was in heaven.

"Do me a favor?" she asked.

"Anything," I answered. And I meant it.

"As your friend."

Uh-oh.

"I've noticed that you don't seem to have much of a social life."

"Yeah?"

"I think you need a girlfriend."

Well, wasn't that a punch to the gut.

"You're a good looking man." She paused and looked at me. "A *very* good looking man. You're also a good man. I know women in general must love you. Now I realize you aren't the type of guy who plays around."

I'll play around with you.

"But you should at least find someone to socialize with so that you aren't alone."

We walked quietly for a while as I let what she'd said sink in. As I did, my mind raced. I wanted her to understand. But I didn't like talking about my time in Vietnam.

Most soldiers don't.

But I decided to tell her.

"In 1967 I was deployed with nine other United States Navy SEALs along the Rach Bau Bong River in Vietnam. We'd set up an ambush. I had 'Big Momma,' my Stoner 63 machine gun with me. I had already killed numerous times with it.

"We waited for hours along the riverbank. Finally a sampan came drifting silently down the river. I could see three North Vietnam Army Soldiers in green uniform on board. One was standing in the front, one standing in the rear steering the boat in the current, and one was standing next to a small shelter in the middle of the sampan."

I looked over at Leigh. She was looking at me listening intently.

"I realized that there could be more NV inside the little hut. Our LT stepped out from behind some bushes and yelled, 'Come here!'

"The NVA soldiers froze. They were in shock that we'd penetrated so far into their territory.

"'Come here!' the LT screamed again.

"He wanted to take them as prisoners.

"But the VC just looked at us like a bunch of idiots. Then all of a sudden they dove into the water.

"We immediately opened fire.

"At the same time, I noticed someone coming out of the little wooden shelter on the sampan. I wasn't going to let the enemy get off any shots at my brothers. So, as the figure emerged, I fired.

"Too late, I realized that it was a woman carrying a bundle."

I paused as my voice started to crack.

"The woman slumped over in the boat," I continued. "I'd shot her numerous times. Then to my horror, I heard a baby crying."

"Oh, no," Leigh muttered.

"'Don't shoot the sampan!' I screamed, as I ran for the river.

"I dove into the water and swam after the boat. Even amidst the sound of gunfire, I could hear the baby crying. It was screaming bloody murder!"

As we walked, I wiped a tear from my eye.

"I climbed onboard the boat and quickly pulled the dead woman's body back. I saw the now quiet baby. It was naked and I saw that it was a boy. A single bullet had gone through the woman and into the infant. I lifted the child into my arms trying to figure out what to do. It was gasping for breath. I was about to yell, 'Medic!' But the baby stopped breathing."

Leigh and I continued on in silence. Even the crickets seemed to have stopped chirping.

"So that's the reason why you won't allow yourself a life?" Leigh asked gently.

I nodded my head, looked away, and blinked back the tears.

"I'm sorry it happened," Leigh's voice was soft and I could tell she meant it. "But, Gary, it was war. You never would've used deadly force on a woman or child."

"But I did. And all I needed to do was wait a split second."

"Yeah?" she argued. "And then maybe somebody else would've shot them."

I wanted to say, "Better them than me," but I didn't.

Instead, I said, "So I decided to honor them. For the innocent life or lives I took. I'm not entitled to happiness."

"Oh, Gary . . ."

We walked onward in silence.

Well, until the day I find Ms. Right . . .

I looked at her expectantly as if I'd voiced my thought.

"You can't do that," Leigh said. "You've got to forgive your-self." She paused and then said, "It takes courage to forgive one's self."

I nodded my head and smiled. I couldn't let her know she'd broken my heart.

It probably took us about three hours to make it back to Willow's compound. I felt terrible for Leigh. She was walking in work shoes that were all but destroyed.

She never complained though.

"What'll we do?" she asked.

"The first thing I want to do is see if we can find food and water."

"And first aid for your arm."

"Oh yeah, I'd forgotten about it."

The buildings were unlocked and we went into the above ground one first.

The only useful thing we found was a hand-cranked water pump.

We filled our canteens. Then we kept exploring but found nothing that could help us.

"You can't fly a plane can you?" I asked, half-seriously, when we got back outside.

"No. How about you?"

"Naw, unfortunately SEALs 'fight our country's battles not the air, but on land and sea'." I said, butchering *The U.S. Marine Corps Hymn.*

As we continued toward the tunnel that led underground, I noticed tall radio antennae.

"Hopefully, there should be some type of radio down there that we can use to call for help."

"That's good because I can't walk another mile in these shoes!"

We found the radio room. We also found a storeroom filled with food and canned water.

We ate like kings and queens and I managed to get in contact with the authorities, who turned out to be the Colorado State Patrol.

The officer I talked to knew exactly where we were. Apparently it had been a big deal when Willow had bought the land and built his compound. It wasn't so much the complex that was newsworthy but the fact that after it was built, he had the road that ran through the property plowed over and then planted with trees and bushes.

The road that some people had used to travel here and there had disappeared in no time.

The locals had called it a "rich man's folly". Willow hadn't wanted people to be able to get to him if Armageddon occurred. The woods acted as a natural barrier to keep people away.

As it turned out, the only way in and out of our location was either by foot or airplane.

I told the officer about Willow's little human hunting game and his death.

"Well, that changes everything from a rescue mission to a murder investigation."

Oh, great!

But I knew better.

"Okay," I said. "But can we get word out to someone that my friend here is all right? She has a family and they must be worried sick!"

The state police did better than that. They patched Leigh into a phone line so she could talk to her husband.

Within the hour, the state police had flown in on a helicopter.

One of the officers stayed behind and took our statements while two other state troopers flew to the cabin and then went to examine Willow's body.

When the officers came back they looked at me guardedly.

"That was a rather disturbing sight," one of them said.

"I had to do what I had to do," I answered.

"It was either us or him," Leigh said, pointing to my blood soaked shirt. "He said he killed for a hobby! He said he's killed several people."

After a few more questions, we finally boarded the chopper. When the helicopter lifted off, I couldn't help but breathe a bit easier. As I looked down at where we'd been, I couldn't help but marvel how such beauty could hide such hell.

I looked over at Leigh and smiled. Somehow we had made it!

We flew into Colorado Springs and were taken to state patrol headquarters.

There, they checked our backgrounds. And after another cursory investigation, we were allowed to leave. Before we did though, they took our contact information in case they had any more questions.

At the station, Leigh called her husband and had him wire some money. She had him send some extra for me too. She said I could owe her.

We were dropped off at a nearby hotel. Leigh and I grabbed a room together.

We needed to clean up.

Leigh showered first. By the time I got out, she had us on a flight that was leaving in a couple of hours.

Leigh went out and bought me a sweatshirt to put over my blood stained Tee-shirt.

It read, *"I like being on top!"*

Under that was a picture of a mountain climber standing on a snow-capped peak.

Below that it read: COLORADO.

"Really?" I asked about the double-entendre.

"Hey, if the shoe fits," Leigh retorted with a smile.

Finally, that night as the sun set in Colorado, Leigh and I found ourselves sitting in an airliner, winging our way back home.

F O R T Y - T W O

Ring.

Joe looked over at the phone and slowly reached for it.

Ring.

"Detective Wilson," Joe said in a weary voice.

He'd just sat down after being out all day on another case. Joe pushed his fedora up on his head, revealing a sweaty band of dampness matting down his gray hair.

"Detective, this is George Ellerton. Leigh is all right!"

Joe perked up in his chair like he'd just been goosed. "And Gary?" he asked hopefully.

"He's all right too."

Joe closed his eyes. *Thank God.*

He took a deep breath and exhaled. Tension escaped his body like air from a balloon.

Suddenly Joe felt very tired, but grateful.

I couldn't have handled losing Gary after losing my boy . . .

"What happened?" Joe asked.

George told him all that he knew.

"And Leigh is hoping to catch the first flight home," he finished.

"Thank you so much for calling, Mr. Ellerton."

They hung up and Joe hit his intercom button.

"Yes?" a female voice answered.

"Is Estes here?"

"No, sir. He's out on patrol."

"Have dispatch radio him. Have them tell him Steel is safe."

[249]

"Yes, sir. That's good news."

"Indeed. Thank you."

Joe reached down and pulled a phonebook out from the bottom of his desk. He flipped through the pages at the front and found the area code for Colorado Springs. He dialed it and then the number for information. A moment later, he was on the line with the Colorado State Patrol.

"I'd like to speak to someone about the Gary Steel kidnapping."

Joe had called to get information, and also to vouch for his friend.

Joe talked to the officer in charge. He didn't learn much and he was relieved to find he didn't need to stick up for Gary.

In the end, Joe hung up and grabbed his coat.

It was time to head home and spend time with his wife.

FORTY-THREE

When we landed at Dulles International Airport, George Ellerton was waiting for us.

He told me how Joe had been worried and I felt like a world class dope. I should've called him.

I was so distracted that I didn't think anyone would notice I was missing. I hadn't even remembered that my car was at the Ellerton house.

Jeepers!

Don't get old kids!

On the way, we gave George a blow-by-blow account of the affair.

In the end he was astonished. And by the way he grabbed his wife's hand and held it, I could tell he was glad to have Leigh back.

I'm good at that.

It was a little after 5 A.M. when we finally pulled up to the Ellerton house in Fairfax Station.

It seemed like a week since we'd been there.

As we climbed out of the car, George said, "I'll go inside and check on the kids. Then I'll get you your keys and wallet."

That left Leigh and me standing outside.

Off on the horizon, Venus shone brightly.

"Well . . ." Leigh said.

"Well, it was a hell of a time," I replied.

"Thank you for taking care of me."

"Thank you for saving my life."

She smiled and laughed. "Anytime."

Then she stepped forward and gave me a heartfelt hug. Then, to my surprise, she kissed me on the check.

Be still my heart.

"I guess I'll talk to you soon," she said as she stepped back.

"Err, yeah, I'll let you know what's going on with Becky's case."

Leigh looked up at me. Even in the dark her eyes glistened. "Good night."

"Night."

I watched her walk inside. A moment later, George came back outside.

"Here you go," he said as he handed me my things.

Then he stuck his hand out and I shook it.

"Thank you for taking care of Leigh. She wouldn't have made it without you."

"I wouldn't have made it without her."

He nodded his head and headed inside.

I hopped into my Corvette and fired her up.

Even though it was early in the morning, I decided to drive to Joe's house.

When I pulled up in front of his house it was still dark.

I'll give him a few minutes.

I closed my eyes for just a moment. The next thing I knew that was a rapping at my door.

I looked and saw Joe standing there in his bathrobe.

"Come on in," he said. "Carolyn's making some coffee. I'll get you a soda."

Joe knew I liked my caffeine cold. I didn't drink coffee.

I got out of the car and, to my surprise, Joe gave me a bear hug.

He looked up at me. "You should've called."

"I know. I blew it. I'm sorry."

Joe stared strangely at me for a moment.

"Do you have a hickey?" Joe asked.

"Huh? What?"

I'd forgotten about the mark on my neck from carrying Leigh up the tree.

I wonder if George saw it.

"I'll tell you about it inside."

And, for the second time that day, I regaled Joe and Carolyn with the story of my adventures.

When I told Joe that the guy claimed he'd killed before, he said he'd look into the unsolved murders.

When I was through, Joe just shook his head. "You get yourself into the worst circumstances."

"What can I say? I'm just a victim of circumstance."

I smiled my most disarming smile.

Carolyn laughed and Joe said, "Nah. You're a troublemaker."

"Any word on the Whitfield case?" I asked, changing subjects.

Joe brought me up to date with all he knew.

Suddenly I wasn't so tired.

"I want to go with you guys tonight."

Joe looked at me. I thought he was going to say no. But he knew I wasn't going to be satisfied by that.

Maybe he'll say the F.B.I. will say no.

"Sure. Like I have a choice in the matter."

I smiled.

"But I want you to have someone take a look at that gunshot wound."

"No problem," I said, standing up.

I'm 'someone'.

"Give me a time and place to meet tonight," I said.

"I'll leave you a message by three."

I started for the door.

"Hey, Gary," Joe called after me.

I stopped and turned around.

"Nice sweatshirt."

Huh? Oh crap! I like being on top.

"Umm, thanks," I managed to reply.

"And welcome home," he concluded.

I smiled. "Thanks."

I went to my car and headed home.

When I was a SEAL I used to be able to sleep anywhere, anyhow.

You had to.

But as a civilian I'd lost that talent. I was used to sleeping in a nice warm bed.

I'd dozed a little on the flight home. However, by the time we landed, I was exhausted.

When I got home, I looked at the wound. It probably needed to be stitched up. Instead, I put some antibiotic on it, taped it together the best I could, and finally wrapped it.

Then, I gratefully dove into bed and hit the sack.

I had to be ready for whatever the night might bring.

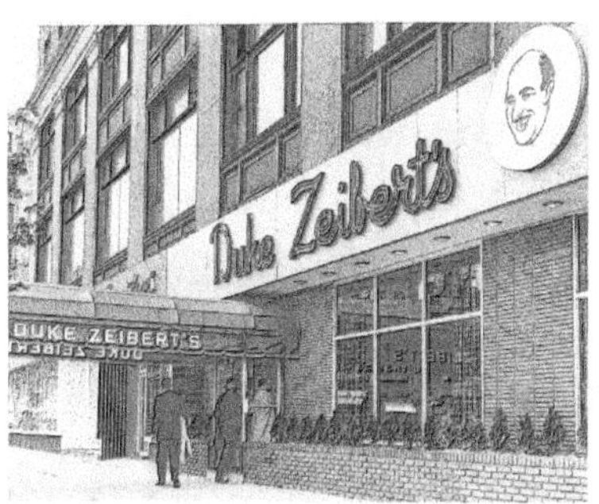

FORTY-FOUR

My phone rang at three o'clock that afternoon.

"Hello?" I croaked in a groggy voice.

I'd been out like a light!

"Gary, you can meet me at the station around seven o'clock."

"Sounds good. Thanks."

I hung up, rolled over, and closed my eyes. I was out again within seconds.

I woke up around 5:30. Feeling like I'd been drugged, I staggered into the bathroom and took a long, hot shower.

As I toweled off and shaved, I threw in a frozen pizza in the oven.

I guzzled down a Mountain Dew to kick start the caffeine and worked on rewrapping my wound.

By 6:55 I was at the Springfield Station of the Fairfax County Police Department.

Of course, Joe was already sitting in his car in the parking lot, waiting.

I popped into the passenger's seat.

Joe took one look at me. I must have still had lines on my face. "Morning, sleeping beauty," he joked.

"Hey, old man," I returned, tongue-in-cheek.

Pretty witty comeback, huh?

"What's the plan?"

"F.B.I. agent Bob Shaw is putting a wire on Drew Harrison as we speak. Right now he's out at the Harrisons' house in Silver Spring. Drew's then going to grab the Metro into D.C. The senator is having an employee dinner at Duke Zeibert's."

"Wow. Nice."

Duke's restaurant had first opened in 1950. To steal a line from the old time radio show, *Duffy's Tavern*, it was the place "where the elite meet to eat". President Harry S. Truman and FBI Director J. Edgar Hoover had dined there. Other patrons included President Clinton, assorted Kennedys, as well as multiple celebrities of note, including talk show host Larry King.

I had to smile. Larry's radio show had gotten me through many late-night stakeouts.

In 1980, the restaurant's original building had been torn down and Duke retired. But playing golf and riding horse-back finally bored him. In 1983, he opened up a new Duke Zeibert's on the second level of the Washington Square building at Connecticut Avenue and L Street NW.

That's where Joe and I headed.

By the time we got there, we found a black van with tinted windows parked out front.

It was obviously a Fed vehicle. But this was D.C. and hardly unusual.

We had to park in a garage a few blocks away and then hike back to Duke's.

Joe walked up to the back of the van. He looked around. There were plenty of people about, but they were in their normal "hurry up" city mindset.

Joe did the "Shave and a haircut, two bits," knock on the back of the paneled door.

A moment later the door opened and we climbed in.

Bob Shaw and another agent were inside.

With the two of us entering, things got a bit crowded inside the van.

"Joe, Gary, this is special agent Elaine Taylor. Elaine, this is Detective Joe Wilson and Gary Steel."

We exchanged greetings and shook hands.

Taylor was a petite brunette dressed in a black pants suit with a white blouse. Her hair was neatly cut shoulder length. She wore only the slightest hint of makeup.

Very professional.

If I had to guess, she was in her late twenties.

"Drew arrived just a few minutes ago," Shaw said.

He had a pair of headphones on and was sitting on a small stool next to a slow moving reel-to-reel tape recorder.

Taylor sat next to him. She also had a headset on.

Joe and I took our seats on the floor.

A fan ran, trying to keep things cool in the van.

I settled in for a long, boring few hours. And I was right.

Private investigating at its best!

Drew didn't talk a lot to his fellow workers. I guess being the new kid on the block was hard all over.

Finally though, the senator approached Drew.

By now Shaw had put things on loudspeaker.

"Some of us are heading over to Roger Penn's place for a nightcap. I expect you to come."

"Okay," Drew said softly.

"And don't worry about transportation. Metro will be closed. I'll make sure you get home. Okay?"

"Yes, sir."

"Sound good?"

"Yes."

"You've done well as my intern, Drew. You stick with me and you'll have a bright future ahead of you."

I could just picture a scared Drew shaking his head.

Things were quiet for a while. Then we heard the senator talking to the whole room.

"Excuse me. Everybody."

You could hear people hushing each other, calling for quiet.

"I've got something to say. Duke is kicking us out of here."

There was a chorus of "Aww".

"Yes, yes, I know. Does everybody have their drinks we just handed out?"

A bunch of "Yeses" echoed through the room.

"A toast! To the best damn employees a senator ever had the privilege of working with! Cheers!"

"Cheers!"

Clinking glasses.

"Now head home. And if you shouldn't be driving, take a cab. It's on me. Just bring your receipts in on Monday."

We heard cheers and goodbyes.

"Drew, you're with me."

I recognized the voice.

"That's Roger Penn," I said.

Drew was on the move.

As there was small talk about whether Drew had enjoyed the party, I said, "I know where Penn lives, a ritzy apartment building in Georgetown. Joe, maybe we should go get your car and try to beat them there."

"Sounds good."

"He lives at—"

"We've got his address," Shaw said. "Thanks."

Joe and I climbed out.

"We'll see you there," Shaw said as Taylor got into the driver's seat and started up the van.

The streets and sidewalks were fairly deserted as Joe and I ran back to his car.

We got out of the garage in a flash and I gave Joe directions. We were the first to get to Penn's apartment. We parked down the street and got out of the car.

We stayed in the shadows as I guided Joe to the building.

Not long afterwards, a car appeared at the end of the street. We watched as it turned into a parking lot that led to the back of the apartment.

"It's Penn and Harrison," Joe said.

I'd recognized them too.

Once they were off the street, another vehicle approached.

It was the van. They parked in front of the building next to Penn's apartment.

We crept up on the van and Joe gave the knock again.

The door flew open and just like that we were back inside.

"Drew told Penn he didn't feel right," Shaw said. "He said he felt dizzy and sleepy."

"They drugged him," I said, stating the obvious.

"Yep. His speech was slurred," Taylor agreed.

Shaw continued, "Penn told him he'd probably just had too much to drink and that he could sleep it off at his place. Drew told him he hadn't had anything until the champagne toast at the end. So obviously that's when they did it."

"They probably used the rape drug flunitrazepam, also known as Rohypnol," Taylor explained. "It's a benzodiazepine used to treat severe insomnia and assist with anesthesia."

I could tell Taylor could've continued on the subject. However, at that moment, another set of car lights appeared on the street.

Silently, we watched it approach.

It was a stretch limousine and it pulled up in front of Penn apartment.

The senator had arrived!

FORTY-FIVE

Drew Harrison had been able to walk from the car. But he was definitely out of it. Inside the apartment, Roger Penn had guided the shaky intern into the guest bedroom.

Roger's family had left earlier that day for the beach. Penn would join them in Ocean City the next day.

"Here," he said quietly to the intern. "Let's take your suit jacket off."

Drew complied as Penn peeled it off like an onion.

Buzz!

Penn walked over to the intercom.

"Yes?"

"Let me in."

Roger immediately recognized the commanding voice of the senator.

He pressed a button.

Bizzzz!

Frank Lindsey came in the front door of the apartment building.

He entered the elevator and pushed the button for the third floor. Once the doors opened, the senator walked with a sense of purpose down the hallway to Penn's apartment. The door had been left open a crack and Lindsey pushed his way inside with a flourish.

He was excited.

He turned and locked the front door.

He knew exactly where Roger and Drew were. It wasn't his first time doing this.

He dropped his thousand dollar suit jacket over the over-stuffed sofa in the living room and then hustled into the guest bedroom.

Roger had laid the boy down on his back and was taking his shoes off.

The senator walked in and looked at the boy. "How long will he be out for?"

"The usual. About an hour."

"I've wanted to be with him from the second I saw him," the senator said as he loosened his tie. "This is going to be great! Look at how pretty he is."

Then talking to Drew he said, "Have you ever been with a man?"

The senator bent down and started to rub Drew's crotch.

As he felt the boy he said, "He's hung."

With the excitement of unwrapping a present, the senator started to unbutton Drew's shirt.

"I can handle it from here," instructed the senator.

Penn understood and started for the door.

"Wh-what's this?" The senator stammered. "He's wearing—"

FORTY-SIX

"—a wire!"

When I heard those words, I shot out the back of the van like a bat out of hell.

"Gar—" Joe called out.

It had taken me all I had inside to stay back when I heard the hung comment. The mental picture of the senator molesting Drew made me sick.

Now I let that fury tear through my veins like a locomotive as I bolted for the apartment.

I knew as a group we'd never get into the building fast enough. We'd have to buzz an apartment that wasn't Penn's and then waste precious time identifying ourselves.

Instead, I ran for the left side of the building. When I got there I started climbing up the decorative corners like it was a ladder.

I was concentrating so hard on what I was doing, I didn't feel the pain in my shoulder. I also didn't hear the sounds of Taylor, Shaw, and Joe pouring out of the van double-time and sprinting for the front of the apartment building.

I made it up the side of the building in no time and hopped onto Penn's deck.

I looked through the sliding glass door.

The senator was hurriedly walking into the living room.

I reached for the door. I was hoping that when you lived on the third floor you didn't bother to lock it.

I was right.

The door slid open.

The senator looked up at me startled.

"What?"

He grabbed his suit jacket and slipped it on, heading for the front door.

I stepped on the coffee table and jumped over the couch. With a few quick steps I got past the senator and got to the door first.

I turned and blocked it from the man.

"Get out of my way!" he demanded. "Do you know who I am? I'm a United States senator! You can't touch me!"

Oh, you should never tell me that.

Without another thought, I punched him.

I punched him as hard as I could in the gut. I punched him for every perverted act he'd ever done to an innocent.

Then another thought rocketed through my mind. It made my temper boil. I thought of the fucking high and mighty politicians who betrayed their purpose, which was to serve this country and not themselves.

The fucking liars!

In general I hated liars. To me they were nothing but cowards!

My fist reared back, ready to fire.

But by this time, the prune-faced Lindsey had doubled over and fell to the ground in a heap. He rolled back and forth on the floor, groaning in anguish and gasping for air.

"Don't *ever* tell me what I can and cannot do, asshat!" I growled in a voice that even scared me.

Careful, don't lose it! I thought, trying to control myself.

I was on the edge.

I suddenly wished I was in the woods of Colorado. I wanted to destroy this piece of shit.

Would I kill again?

But I was in civilization.

I desperately wanted to kick the poor excuse of a man in the face. It certainly wouldn't have hurt his looks!

But I reached deep down inside and trembling, I found patience and compassion.

I kicked him in the shin instead.

He let out a bloodcurdling scream.

"Oops! I'm sorry," I said, as I went over to the intercom on the wall and pushed the button that would allow Joe and the others to come in through the front door.

Watching Lindsey still rolling around on the floor, I opened the front door and left it open.

Then I knelt down and stuck my face into the senator's. "Don't try going anywhere or I will truly hurt you," I spat. "Understand?"

The piece of shit weakly nodded his head.

Satisfied that the dishonorable Senator Frank Lindsey wasn't going anywhere, I hurried through the apartment looking for Drew.

It didn't take me long to find him. He was half-dressed, lying on top of a bed.

Roger Penn stood next to him.

He was holding a gun and it was pointing at me.

FORTY-SEVEN

"Whoa-whoa, big fella," I said as I threw my hands up. "The authorities are on their way up."

"That's what I thought," he said calmly.

He put the gun in his mouth and, before I could do anything, pulled the trigger.

I braced myself for the sound and the gory sight of a man's brains blown all over the place.

But the gun didn't fire.

Penn pulled the gun out of his mouth and stared at it in disbelief. "Fuckin' wife!" he exclaimed as he threw the gun at me. "She emptied the gun because of the kids!"

I swatted the pistol away like it was an annoying fly and stepped closer to him.

"Look," I said, my mind whirling. "If you help me put the senator away, I'll try to help you out and get your sentence reduced."

Now, of course, I didn't have the authority to make that kind of offer. But he wasn't to know.

Penn sat down on the edge of the bed and put his head in his hands.

"I'm glad this is over with," I heard him sob.

A moment later the Cavalry arrived.

FORTY-EIGHT

Over the next few months Washington was awash in scandal.

The senator was arrested and his trial was must-see TV.

As I watched the proceedings, I thought about Lindsey. I was sure that the selfish piece of shit justified whatever he wanted to do by saying he worked hard for his constituency. Therefore, since he worked hard, what was wrong with him blowing off a little steam? Then, I could just hear him say the words that make me cringe every time I hear them: "I deserve it."

Whoever deserves anything!

In the end, with the help of Roger Penn, Lindsey was convicted and sentenced.

As was Mitchell Jones. He was convicted of the murder of Cody Whitfield and the attempted murder of Becky Whitfield as well as various other drug possession charges thrown in for good measure.

Even though he was instrumental in helping to get both convictions, Roger Penn was still sentenced ten years in prison.

Unlike the others, he'd at least have a chance for a new life once he got out of prison.

The senator, or should I say the convicted pedophile, would've gotten his due justice in prison However, because of who he was, he was kept isolated from the general population.

It must be nice to be rich and have friends.

There was an emergency election to fill his spot in the Senate and I'm happy to report a woman won.

The state will be better off.

Meanwhile, Joe found a 1987 video of a woman being strangled to death in the basement of an office building. When she was dead, the killer had waved at the video camera and casually walked off.

Even though the murderer was in disguise, Joe had me come in and take a look. From the height, weight, and the way he moved, I knew the killer was indeed Percy Willow.

Autumn had come to Northern Virginia. The air was crisp with possibilities and the sound of school children's laughter. My upper arm had healed and I was back to working out full-time.

One morning, I had just finished a particularly heavy workout and I was in the kitchen. making myself a snack. when I heard the doorbell to my office go off.

I grabbed a tee-shirt and pulled it over my wet body as I made my way downstairs.

When I got to the reception area, I saw an attractive woman standing at the entrance.

I opened the door and let her in.

It took me a moment to recognize her.

"Becky. Hi. How're you doing?"

"I'm doing very well, thank you!"

She looked and sounded wonderful.

"Please, take a seat."

She sat down while I grabbed a seat behind the reception desk.

I looked at the two bullet holes in the desktop.

Yep. It adds character.

I looked at Becky. She'd lost weight since the last time I'd seen her. She also appeared younger.

But the biggest difference was her face. She was always pretty. Now though, she was absolutely beautiful. Her eyes sparkled and I could tell that she was clean.

"I just wanted to stop by and give you this," she said as she reached into her oversize purse.

She pulled out a small Tupperware container and handed it to me.

"I can never repay you for all that you've done. All I can do is show you my gratitude. I made you some chocolate chip cookies."

She leaned toward me and held them out.

I stood up and reached for them.

"It's a small token of thanks for saving my life." She paused and looked me in the eyes. "In more ways than one."

"It was my pleasure," I said sincerely. "Thank you for the cookies. I love chocolate chip."

"I know. Leigh told me."

She smiled again and I was once again taken aback by her beauty.

"I've just gotten back from the Betty Ford Center."

"Rehab?" I asked.

"Yes. It was the best thing I've ever done. I'm clean. And God willing, I will remain so."

"That's wonderful!" I replied.

"I'm going for joint custody of my kids."

"Well, that's great. I wish you well."

And I did.

"I also met a man," she declared excitedly.

"Oh?"

"His name is Lucas Starr."

I recognized the name. He was a multi-millionaire who lived in McLean.

"I think he's the one."

She smiled and blushed. It was as adorable as a kitten falling over!

Well, good for her.

The following morning, I was getting my running in when I stopped and watched a group of twenty-somethings playing basketball.

They'd be about the same age as the baby I killed . . .

My mind flashed back to the familiar scene and I cringed.

All these years later it was still hard.

I heard the words of Leigh in my head.

Forgive yourself.

Suddenly I was overcome with emotion.

I hid my face in my hand and looked at the ground. Then I cried like a fucking baby.

I cried for the child. But this time I also cried for me.

I'd spent twenty-six years browbeating and whipping myself emotionally.

Leigh had been right. It had to stop!

It's done. No more!

I realized I might have been standing around too long at the pickup game. I turned and left. I didn't want people thinking I was some type of a perv.

I ran home.

Sometimes in life you run into someone who is really important to you. They change your life and make it better.

And sometimes that person can't stay in your life . . .

But that's okay. They helped to make you the person you are today.

Thanks Leigh.

That night I went to bed. And I slept fine.

If you enjoyed:

STEEL'S METTLE

Don't miss:

STEEL'S TREK

The fourth novel featuring:

Gary Steel, P.I.

Coming soon!

An Excerpt From:

Steel's Trek

TEXT BY C. EMERSON

PROLOGUE

1989

Carlos Rodriquez smiled, his yellow teeth glistening with moisture.

He was actually salivating!

The *Padrino* (GODFATHER) of the *El Dolor* (THE PAIN) drug cartel was looking through a dirty, six by three inch window.

He was horny.

Carlos was attracted to the woman and her "little girl" like body.

I'm going to enjoy fucking her.

The object of his desire was tied up, blindfolded, and had a pillowcase pulled over her head. She lay on the floor of an old, rusted metal shipping container.

The young woman was sobbing. One of Carlos's men had just brought her in from a local bar. She'd ordered a cab. But instead of taking the young woman to her hotel in San Felipe, the driver had brought her out to the boondocks—to hell.

San Felipe was a popular spring break spot for residents of the western United States due to its many tourist attractions. It was a place where nightclubs and bars dotted the beach areas.

El Dolor had recently branched out from drugs to kidnapping rich Americans and holding them for ransom. This girl, Julia Marvin, was a college junior at UCLA. She was the daughter of a powerful business mogul from the United States: one J. T. Marvin, IV.

Julia Marvin was going to be worth a pretty peso. Lots of them!

Carlos was a short, powerful man, built like a bull. He was in his late-thirties and had short dark hair with flecks of gray starting to show. Carlos was the proud owner of a crooked nose that had been hit one time too many. In his mind it was a badge of honor, showing how many men he'd taken down with his fists.

Never had the term, "You should see the other guy," been more appropriate.

A single light bulb hung from the ceiling, dully illuminating the interior.

There was a flat mattress on the dirty floor and that was it.

Carlos reached into his pocket and pulled out a key to the Master Lock that was on the door.

The container itself was inside an old abandoned factory. There were armed men all around the place making sure that rivals or *Federales* didn't show up unexpectedly.

That wouldn't be easy in the middle of nowhere.

In the old factory, the gang members of the cartel could sort their drugs and work in private.

Music constantly blared near the old shipping container so that their "guests" couldn't hear what was happening outside. As an added bonus, it added to the prisoner's distress never getting any quiet.

For the moment, Carlos had turned the music off.

He quickly opened the container and unbolted the heavy metal door.

It squeaked loudly in protest.

He normally would've had the hinges oiled, but he felt the sound helped to unnerve the prisoner.

And he was right.

"Who's there?" Julia yelled. "Let me go! You have no idea who my father is!"

"Actually I do," Carlos replied softly with a slight accent.

He'd gone to school in the United States.

Carlos walked over and took the pillowcase from her head.

"That is why you're here," he finished.

Julia started to panic. He had allowed her to see his! He was going to kill her!

"Relax," Carlos said. "You are safe . . . for the moment."

He smiled, flashing his yellow teeth.

If he was trying to calm Julia, it wasn't working. She became more alarmed. Or maybe she could read his mind.

Carlos ran his hand gently along her face.

"You're very pretty," he said.

Julia closed her eyes, tears started to roll down her cheeks.

"No. Please don't."

"Having you here and not doing anything would be such a waste," he said as he started to unbutton her blouse.

Carlos could feel his heart start to pound faster as a tingle of excitement started to grow below.

Julia turned away, "No!"

Carlos lost his patience. He took two hands and ripped her shirt open.

Julia was flat and because of that, tended to go braless.

Her tiny white tits were exposed.

She tried to scramble away.

Carlos grabbed her by the throat and said, "We can do this the hard way, or easy. And I don't care. But you *are* going to do this."

Then he struck her in the face.

Julia cried out in pain. Then she just lay there quietly as he pulled her pants and then her little panties off.

Carlos rolled her onto her back.

He positioned himself on his knees. Julia closed her eyes as he undid his belt and unzipped his fly.

He pulled his pants down, exposing his thick but short manhood. He was fully erect.

"Spread your legs," he ordered.

At first she did nothing.

"Spread your legs, dammit!"

She pulled them apart.

He smiled as he looked down at her neatly trimmed pussy.

"I'm going to enjoy this," he said as he positioned himself over her.

She's gonna feel so good.

He looked down and grabbed his little erection. He started to guide it in.

"No!" Julia yelled.

Crack!

Carlos felt pain as his nose exploded into pieces.

Julia had jerked her head upwards, violently. She'd used her forehead as a weapon and Carlos's nose had been broken yet again.

"Bitch!" he shrieked as his cock immediately went flaccid in his hands.

Blood started pouring down his face and splattering on Julia.

She closed her eyes, preparing herself for the beating that was sure to come.

Carlos balled up his fist and was prepared to strike. But suddenly he was lifted into the air.

Julia opened her eyes in surprise and realized that another man had pulled her attacker off of her.

Carlos was confused as he felt himself torn from the woman.

He saw it was Pablo.

"*¿Qué?*" Carlos demanded angrily.

But he wasn't able to say anything else as Pablo punched him in the gut.

Stunned, Carlos doubled over and fell to the ground.

"You will die for this!" Carlos gasped as anger boiled over.

"No, *amigo*, you will," Pablo said flatly, looking down at the man.

Carlos had been the *Padrino* for so long, he didn't understand what it was like to be ignored. He was used to his every word, his every whim, being respected.

"Pablo! What is the meaning of this?"

Carlos was on his knees. He was doubled over in pain holding his stomach. He was hard, his hairy butt facing Julia.

Pablo didn't answer the man. Instead, he pulled his hunting knife from the sheath attached to his belt.

Pablo slowly approached the man.

Carlos realized what was happening.

"No!" he shrieked

He threw his hands up to protect himself, but Pablo's blow landed straight and true.

Carlos's eyes widened horror as he fell to the ground. He saw the knife sticking out of his chest, then nothing.

He was dead before he landed.

"Get him out of here!" Pablo snapped, directing two men who had been standing in the doorway.

They ran in, grabbed Carlos, and dragged him out.

Pablo turned his attention to Julia.

"I'm sorry you had to see that," he said sincerely.

The man had been raised in the United States and only had a slight Spanish accent. That gave Julia hope.

"Let me introduce myself," he continued. "My name is Pablo Sanza, the new *Padrino* of *El Dolor*."

"Thank you! Thank you so much!" Julia said sincerely.

Pablo smiled. He had nice white teeth.

He was a good looking man, tall, lean, and muscular. He was just nineteen years old and now he was the head of one of the most violent gangs in Mexico.

"My *amigo*," he said as he thumbed in the direction of the dead man, "Carlos was getting soft, so I decided to take over."

He smiled again.

Soft? Julia thought.

Suddenly a chill ran through the girl.

Pablo came towards her. His smile was different.

"No-no, pleaseeeee!" she screamed as she tried to crab-walk away.

Pablo grabbed her by the throat and pinned her down. He ripped her top and pulled her pants and panties off. Then he climbed on top of the girl and raped her again and again.

ONE

September, 1996

It was 0900.

Ring!

That was my house phone. I picked it up.

"Hello?"

"I need your help."

"When?"

"Now."

"Where?"

"Here. And bring your passport."

"I'm on my way."

We hung up.

I went into the guest bedroom and grabbed my old Navy SEAL duffel bag. Then I went into my room and started jamming clothes and toiletries into it.

On a whim, I grabbed a pair of old surplus store fatigues and combat boots.

I guess some habits die hard.

I pushed a hidden button on my bedroom wall. There was a slight click and then a panel of drywall slid silently to the side. I stepped inside what I like to call The Pit.

It was a secret room I'd built in my house. It was the nerve center for my detective agency. I kept important things in there, including documents, guns, high-tech surveillance equipment, as well as other necessities.

In this case, a safe.

The room was small, only about six foot by twelve. The walls were lined with lead so that sensors couldn't pick up my heat signature when I was inside.

The lead also served to fireproof the room.

The room also had openings to the garage and the roof.

I opened the safe and pulled out my passport and two thousand dollars in cash. I slipped the money into my pants pockets.

I guess I'd better stop and explain a few things right here.

My name is Gary Steel. Like I said, I'm a private investigator. I'd just turned fifty years old a couple of months earlier. Aging used to bother me. But turning fifty changed my attitude. I was just glad to be alive. A lot of my friends hadn't made it to fifty. Hell, many didn't even make it to twenty-five!

Despite my age, I manage to stay fit. I'm a hair under 6'4" in height and I weigh about 225. I'm proud to say they are lean, muscular pounds. In fact, I'm stronger now than I was in my Navy SEAL days, back when I served two tours in Vietnam. But I may be a step slower.

Maybe.

I only have two real friends in this world. And I consider myself lucky to have that many. One is Joe Wilson who's a police detective with the Fairfax County Police Department. The other had just called. His name was Larry Collins.

Or maybe I should say, Vice Admiral Lawrence Collins.

Yes, my friend has three stars.

Me? I got out of the Navy long before he did. However, I'm proud to say I made the rank of Master Chief Petty Officer before I retired.

Larry lives south of Imperial Beach just south of San Diego, California. He lives there with his wife, Lori, and their three kids, Allison, Larry, who they call Junior, and Carly.

On the other hand, I live alone in the suburbs of Washington D.C.

Larry said he needed me. So I'm hopping on the first plane I can to the west coast.

After packing, I made a quick call to the post office. I told them to hold my mail. Then I made sure the house was locked up before I went down into the garage.

I have two cars. My baby is a red, 1991, Chevrolet Corvette ZR-1. The other one is a 1989, neon-green, Ford Taurus wagon.

Can you guess which one I use to follow subjects?

Yes, the Taurus was my car of choice when I don't want to call attention to myself. It was also my preferred car now, since I didn't want to leave my Vette at the airport parking garage for who knew how long.

I pulled out and headed to Dulles International Airport in Chantilly, Virginia.

I chose that over Reagan National Airport in Arlington because it has more flights and my chances of getting to California were better.

I parked my car in the long-term parking lot and walked to the terminal.

I looked at the departures. There was a nonstop flight to San Diego leaving in two hours.

Perfect. I hope there's a seat.

I went to the ticket counter and luck was with me.

I was charged for a one-way ticket and walked to the gate to wait for departure.

It was 15:30 when I arrived in San Diego.

I grabbed a cab and, an hour later, I was walking up the side-walk to the Collins' residence.

Not bad, I thought, looking at my watch. Ten and a half hours after the call.

I pressed the doorbell.

A moment later I heard the sound of someone walking and then Larry opened the door.

One look at his face and I knew something was wrong— terribly wrong.

"Gary," he said as he threw open his arms.

I dropped my duffel and gave him a bear hug.

Larry was a few years older than I was. He was a big, barrel-chested black man who was as strong as an ox. His shaved head only added to the intimidation factor.

"You've gained some weight," I said, as we broke the hug. "You look like the Pillsbury Doughboy."

"Only darker," he agreed. "And that's what happens when you're stuck behind a desk, working." He patted his belly. "Instead of waltzing around pretending to be Sherlock Holmes," he quipped. "Get a real job, son."

I smiled. It felt good. We usually gave each other crap and it appeared age hadn't slowed us down.

"Come on in, Gary. Thanks for coming. I appreciate it."

"Of course. I wouldn't wanna be anywhere else."

Larry led me into a comfortable living room.

"It's been a few years since I've been here," I said as I sat down. "I can tell Lori has done a great job keeping it up to date. Knowing you, you'd have nothing but beanbag chairs and milk crates for furniture."

Larry didn't counter punch and that concerned me. I was an easy target with my obvious fashion faux pas.

This is serious.

"Where's Lori?" I asked.

"She's been kidnapped."

"What?" I reacted.

It felt like I'd been punched in the gut.

"She's been kidnapped and being held for ransom."

"When? How?"

"Last Monday she went shopping and never came home. I reported her missing and the next day her car was found in Tijuana."

"Tijuana, Mexico?" I asked dumbly.

Larry nodded his head. "Later that day an envelope arrived on our doorstep. Ally found it and brought it to me."

The kids!

The Collins had three children. Allison, who was nicknamed Ally, was 10; Larry Junior, 15; and Carly, 17.

"Where are the kids?" I asked, concerned.

"They're at Lori's sister's house. They don't know what's happening. They think we both had to go out of town. The two oldest wanted to stay home alone. I said no."

"Good," I said, nodding my head in agreement.

"Here's the letter," Larry said, handing me an oversized envelope by the corner.

I assumed Larry hadn't gone to the police or he wouldn't have the ransom note. They would've taken it as evidence.

I held the envelope carefully and examined it. There was nothing special about it. It was just your run-of-the-mill mustard-colored 9" × 12" reusable clasp Kraft envelope.

I pulled a piece of paper out and examined it. By the print quality I could tell it'd been printed on a dot matrix printer. That and the fact the paper still had the guide holes on the side.

"Very 1980s," I quipped.

It read:

> We have your wife. If you want to see her again, you will give us one million dollars in U.S. currency in $20, $50, and $100s. The bills are to be unmarked and with no sequential numbers.
>
> You have until Saturday, September 7th to raise the money. Then we will contact you with final directions.
>
> Do not go to the police or she's dead.
> We don't really care either way.

Chills ran down my spine. These guys seemed brutal.

I looked at the back of the paper to see if there was anything else on it. There wasn't.

"There's a picture in there," Larry said.

I reached in as a feeling of dread washed over me.

It was a Polaroid picture. It showed Lori, naked, bound and gagged.

I felt my temper start to boil.

"Can you raise that type of money?" I asked.

Larry pointed to the corner. There was a grey Samsonite suitcase standing there.

"Full of green," he said. "Lori and I had put it aside for the kid's college fund at a good rate. We want them to go to the best college they can with money being no object."

I remembered that Larry had inherited a lot of money from his parents a few years ago.

I looked at him.

"I went to the bank today. I'd given them the weekend as a heads up. They didn't like the idea of me withdrawing so much. But they did it."

"So, you are paying the ransom?"

"Yeah. I don't feel like I have a choice. I want my wife back."

I nodded my head.

"You doing okay?" I asked.

"I've been better," he replied sadly. "I'm just scared to death for Lori. She's a good woman and I pray they don't hurt her."

My anger was churning inside of me. I wanted to kill the kidnappers.

"We'll get them, Larry. I promise."

The phone rang and we both stared at it.

"But it's not Saturday yet," I said.

"Welcome to my nightmare."

TWO

Pablo Sanza looked through the small dirty window of the old rusted storage container at the naked Lori Collins.

She's got a good body for someone her age.

Lori had been scared since they'd brought her there. They always were. But she hadn't cried.

That *was* unusual.

Unlike most females that the *El Dolor* kidnapped, Pablo hadn't had his way with Lori.

Yet.

Although he'd never admit it, there was something about this woman that scared him. She had a quiet strength and dignity that unsettled Pablo. She was a proud black woman and deep-down he couldn't wait to be rid of her.

The ransom money can't come quick enough!

"We are dropping her off tonight," Hector Torres yelled over the music as he approached the *Padrino*.

Hector was Pablo's right-hand man, his Lieutenant. He was tall and lean just like his *Padrino*. He'd known Pablo since they were kids. Hector was good-looking and somehow the scar on his check added to his rugged good looks. Women liked him and he liked them back. If you had a problem with Pablo, you had to go through him first. It was something people didn't do, especially after Hector had beaten two men to death with his bare hands.

"I know you want to be rid of her," Hector explained. "I checked on the progress as you directed. Her husband has already withdrawn the money. So I moved the time up for the exchange."

"*Gracias*, Hector!" Pablo said gratefully. "What time?"

"Midnight."

Pablo looked at his watch. They had plenty of time.

"Go ahead and get the plane ready." He paused and looked at his Lieutenant. "Do you want to fuck her before we turn her over?"

Pablo realized he wanted to see this woman pounded into submission.

Hector smiled. "No thank you, *Padrino*. She's too old for me. I like them young. I wouldn't be able to get it up."

Pablo nodded his head while Torres walked off.

Pablo took another peek at the woman. She was working on trying to free her hands.

She won't give up.

He kept watching.

Maybe I should just go in there and teach her some respect, he thought as he grabbed himself between the legs and started to rub. *I'll leave my seed in you bitch. How'd you like that?*

Suddenly, she stopped. It was as if she knew she was being watched. Lori looked up at the small window and scowled, her eyes shooting daggers.

Pablo moved out of her line of sight like a child caught with his hand in the cookie jar. And as he hid behind the door from his captive, all thoughts of raping her vanished.

Yes, it'll be good to be rid of her!